LESSONS
FOR A
CHILD
WHO
ARRIVES
LATE

LESSONS FOR A CHILD WHO ARRIVES LATE

Carlos Yushimito

Translated from the Spanish by
Valerie Miles

TRANSIT
BOOKS

Published by Transit Books
2301 Telegraph Avenue, Oakland, California 94612
www.transitbooks.org

Copyright © Carlos Yushimito 2011
c/o Schavelzon Graham Agencia Literaria
www.schavelzongraham.com
English translation copyright © Valerie Miles 2017

Originally published in Spanish as *Lecciones para un niño que llega tarde*
in 2011 by Duomo Ediciones, Barcelona

ISBN: 978-1-945492-05-1
LIBRARY OF CONGRESS CONTROL NUMBER: 2017953484

DESIGN & TYPESETTING
Justin Carder

DISTRIBUTED BY
Consortium Book Sales & Distribution
(800) 283-3572 | cbsd.com

Printed in the United States of America

9 8 7 6 5 4 3 2 1

TABLE OF CONTENTS

LESSONS
FOR A
CHILD
WHO
ARRIVES
LATE

Seltz

I COULD FEEL HIS SOUR, *cachaça* breath on my ear as I slipped out of my costume in the stockroom. It was Bautista, the manager. His face was dripping sweat. He must have been partying already, I supposed, as usual, the way he screwed up his mouth to fling words at me. It wasn't out of the ordinary for me to be taken with a strange sense of embarrassment. A sneaking sense of guilt. For a few seconds, I felt as though someone were watching two lobsters copulating in slow motion and there I was standing by his side, in front of twenty television screens broadcasting the same image. Slow motion. Very slow motion.

Zé Antuncs says the best sales pitch for an appliance store like ours is to have all the televisions tuned to the Discovery Channel.

"It's like this," he says, "imagine we air a rock concert or a soccer game: parents will associate the television set with drugs or wasted leisure time. If we put a movie on, a fortysomething married woman with university-age children will remember with nostalgia and resentment that her husband rarely takes her to the movies anymore."

Zé Antunes says the educational channels boost the chances of clinching a sale, and it must be true because parents always consider education a good investment, and they'll never skimp when it comes to that.

"That's the sweet spot we have to target: the jugular vein of sales," he declares.

Zé Antunes knows a lot about the animal kingdom, though not as much as he does about sales and marketing. That's why I try to pay attention to what he says, soak up all that wisdom.

With Bautista it's different. Watching his overblown gestures, almost certain his atrophied nose had snorted a good bit of blow that afternoon, I thought about his idea of happiness and the good deal he must have struck with the Draco distributor. Common knowledge says that one thing leads to another. And Bautista really knows the business because his father is the owner and one of the richest and most influential men in Río de Janeiro.

"I have a new get-up for you tonight, Toninho."

Patting me on the back complicitously, Bautista remained alert, not realizing that I had no desire to spend another debauched night at his side. That's why, even though he insisted, I preferred not to raise my head and confirm or deny anything. I just kept on with my whimsical striptease till I recovered my human shape.

He finally gave up. Maybe he was intimidated by my self-possession. He made a gun with his hand, and pulled the trigger in his bloodshot eyes. "I'll wait for you out in the car."

* * *

He was waiting in the hallway, not the car.

"Did you turn off the faucet?" Zé asked.

Yes, I said, but the suspicious prick went to check for himself. He came back soon after, drying his hands.

"A cautious man is worth twenty of his kind," he said.

By now, the sliding gate had sealed the main entrance. The three of us were the only ones left inside, canned between white floor tiles and television screens, all tuned to the same channel. A lion with a fiery mane strode away, wiggling his haunches as he carried off a chunk of groin, while a few hyenas fought over the remains of what had once been a zebra. They ate with ardor, with an African appetite. Bautista and Zé Antunes, paying no attention to me, kept on chatting raucously over by the cash register.

"There's a jacket and some good pomade in the trunk," Bautista said, briefly interrupting their conversation. He gestured with his hands as if his head were a fortune-teller's crystal ball.

"Put it on and get in the car."

He tossed me the keys.

Before I left, I saw Zé slip him a little yellow envelope. It was the kind they used when they squared the monthly accounting. Despite his age, Zé Antunes had the most seniority of anyone in the store; he locks up every night, turns off the equipment, and disconnects the electricity. He's the last to leave and the first to arrive except on Tuesdays, his morning off. In my four years here, I've never once known him to miss a day or take a vacation. I've never heard him complain, curse, or hassle anyone who didn't deserve it.

Really, everyone should try to be like him.

I closed the trunk feeling more upbeat and enthusiastic than before. I slipped into the newly dry cleaned jacket, finished smoothing my hair back with the pomade, and slid into my place in the copilot's seat. I caught a glimpse of myself in the rear-view mirror and wasn't too disgusted. I switched the radio on. Daniela Mercury's voice groaned into the speakers with the same sensuous quality her body had: *Vem ai baile movido a nova fonts de energia. Chacina, política e mídia. Bem perto da casa que eu vivia . . . electrodoméstico . . . eletro-brasil . . .*

Open shirt, brown tweed jacket, slicked black hair. Within minutes I had become a variation on Bautista, somewhat smaller and less elegant. My chest, slightly bared, enjoyed the feeling of the air that gusted in through the window of the Audi. I liked playing the part of the fun-loving guy on a Friday night, out to play, out to release the stress of a deal. I had that troubled, tense quality, as if I could explode at any moment, which is so attractive to women. I scrutinized myself in the window. Over and over, I looked at myself. It did the trick all right: I felt strong, sophisticated. Free of my usual scruffy, bargain-basement clothes, I was a natural lady-killer; that instinct simmered up silently, ready to reveal itself. And yet self-possession held on like a spark of light. Bautista is a rich kid who only engages in sports to compete, not for fun, and decks himself out in pricey clothes I could never afford, not even with five months' salary. He knows how to carry himself; he fits into things easily, both on his body and in life. He has eyes as green as two fireflies aglow in the night and good bones that give off testosterone mixed with the soft aroma of Gucci. If only I could sweet-talk like him, his behavioral determination (as Zé would say), when he wants to get a beautiful girl into bed.

"Tickets?" the big black bouncer says at the door.

He gives me a cheeky scan from head to toe.

"It's okay, Ciro. He's with me."

Bautista knows how to undermine authority with nothing more than his smile. With the membership card, the rest of the doors were opened to us. With an eye on the bouncer's now sweeter airs, I stand tall in my tweed jacket and walk forward confidently. I pass through. Impatient, I feel the pulsing energy that pleasure and rank awaken. Inside there's a chrome-plated corridor; you can intuit the impending explosion that comes with the shock of being swallowed into that throbbing fable of a thousand lives in motion. The lights beckon us like two astronauts lost in space. This is human wealth; the center of power at rest. Although seen from the darkness, there's nothing that differentiates these people from the ones left outside, men and women are only shadows and sparks of themselves; heads and tails of the same coin, though a coin that fetches a very different price.

"They're like drug-sniffing dogs," Bautista says almost screaming as we walk side by side. "They can smell poor people two hundred meters away."

"They must get a lot of practice," I answer, checking my temper. "I see that black guy at the door every day on his way up to São Clemente to sell drugs."

We start making our way when someone approaches us.

"Bautista," the man says.

I watch them embrace and kiss each other on the cheek. He's a skinny type with glasses. Inconsequential.

"Don't tell me you want to keep talking business here."

"As long as we have the same chemistry," he laughs, touching his snout.

He's the Draco distributor.

"Evaristo Rangel." He holds his hand out to me.

"Toninho," I say.

"My cousin Toni," Bautista corrects me, shooting a look of cloaked scorn.

"Oh . . . so you're the famous Toni," Rangel says, taking me in curiously. "The famous Toni," he repeats, this time looking at Bautista. I feel a little stupid, laughing without catching their drift.

A good part of the night will go by in hollow, pointless conversation, stories that nobody will appreciate or even

remember later. Every once in a while they scrape out
three lines of coke and I snort one so as not to ruin the
getup Bautista picked out for me. Well, maybe I snort
more than just one. At this rate, it'll be easy to lie. The
time will come when nothing is real, and they won't be
able to differentiate what they're saying from what I said
that they said. Soon I'll be the funniest guy on Earth,
because that's what they decided. I'll say that sex with
snakes is slow, same as their digestion process, and a pi-
geon screwing is a horrifying thing, they almost literally
pluck their feathers out, the most sadistic and refined animals for pain, especially among themselves. I'll say things
that aren't threatening. I'll laugh at my own jokes, pretending that someone else is the idiot who dances for children in a crocodile costume. They'll laugh. We'll laugh.
I could tell them, without a hint of sarcasm, that they're
a couple of idiots, and still get a good belly laugh out of
them. The game change prompt will come as a surprise
from the chaos. Two brunettes like "Oh my God" will
join the party, bouncing cleavages, thighs, calves, everything about them smelling of sex. When they say hello,
their silky pants lick my leg, and I'll feel the need to do
another line, but there are no more lines for Toninho.
Maybe there's one more for Toni, I'll say to Bautista.
And he'll laugh. And I'll snort it. The Draco distributor
will supply us with caipirinhas and beer. It's the black
bouncer, yes sir, who gets us the coke. The brunettes will

eye me lustily, I know. Shamelessly, I can almost imagine an orgy on the table, and as I move to touch a thigh, Bautista pulls me to the far side of the sofa and tells me he has to take off with Evaristo Rangel.

"You're the best, Toninho. Remind me to give you a raise next month."

I know next month will never come, but I hug him anyway and he pulls himself away softly because one of the brunettes snatches him from behind like a teddy bear. She has a pair of eyes that turn everything to stone. My dick, for starters. My mouth. My self-esteem. I go back to the table alone. Evaristo hugs me and kisses me on the cheek.

"The famous Toni," he says.

And I laugh too, I giggle and hoot as I watch how Bautista and Rangel take off, arm in arm, like two colossal queens. One of the waiters taps me on the shoulder and hands me the yellow envelope Bautista left behind, and I inspect it carefully, and slip it straight into my pocket. If I were a sensible man, being poor as I am, I would hold on to it for a little while, sip my last beer, then head home with an extra month's wages in hand. If I were smart, I would just drain my glass without looking at anyone or anything. But somehow the first beer multiplies miraculously in my hands as I linger at the same table, and my empty glass now filled with a new, radiant magical liquid, and I happen to recognize Julia, oh, the beautiful Julia Oliveira.

* * *

"Have you seen Bautista?" she asks.

I shrug.

"He took off," I say.

I can see her wounded cat pupils dilate in the darkness. I imagine she pulled her hair back to appear dignified in the face of abandonment.

"Asshole," she mumbles, referring to Bautista.

She suddenly turns around and gives me her back.

The second time I catch her hovering around the table. I feel sorry for her. I check out her tits.

"So who are you?" she asks, my curiosity piquing her interest.

"Toni," I lie. "The asshole's cousin."

She laughs, now kittenishly.

"So I suppose you don't know where he went, huh?"

I'm not going to betray my friend.

I say no.

"Course not," she says, taking a seat. "You men always cover for each other when you get into trouble. Must be a gender thing, I guess. An animal instinct like for survival or something. We women, we hold out for the first chance we get to annihilate one another. I mean, why do we do it? Maybe we just evolved quicker than you guys." Her voice breaks, I think she's about to cry. "I don't care that he has other women, as long as he tells me about it, know what I mean?"

But I don't believe her. It's just a ploy to get me to spill information.

We watch the people on the dance floor for a while, and then I feel her eyes on me again.

"You know how to dance, don't you?"

This time I say yes and I'm not lying. I danced for the Escola de Samba Mangueira for five years, till I could no longer live for a year off one month's salary and realized that gigs in sequins would never provide enough to eat. Back then dancing helped me find a job that was above board, and now it would help me land a pretty girl. Who was it who said dancing would never get me anywhere? What did it matter, I told myself: a person is the life they live. I felt lucky for being so agile, for my strong and flexible arms. It was easy for my body to adjust to the peculiar sensuousness Julia gave off; it was easy for me to charge her strong thighs with my own. I pinned her with a professional look, making it clear that we were nothing but a man and a woman doing what they wanted on a dance floor. Nothing else counted. We bumped and grinded until our legs begged for mercy—hers before mine—and we returned to the sofa, exhausted. We were like two lobsters being examined under a hidden camera, I thought: thousands of television sets tuned on us, there's the collusion of a good deal, the happiness of respectable parents. I could feel the next song's red and yellow lights electrifying us again, the gravelly voice of Tim Maia slinking around like a commando in the darkness.

"You sure can dance," she whispered in my ear.

What she wanted to say is "you're an amazing dancer, incredible," but her feminine reserve held her back, something I taught myself to spot and even take some pride in by skimming the gossip magazines in the hair salon.

"Not as good as you are," I lied.

"Now I really hope your cousin doesn't show up, Toninho."

She remembered my name.

We danced the rest of the night. We kissed. I kept count of what was left in the envelope. Making up some excuse, she took me back to her place later. She wanted to know if what they said was true: that people screw like they dance.

"Two wolves who encounter each other outside a neutral territory will inevitably engage in aggressive behavior until one of them prevails. Under these circumstances, the weaker wolf, instead of perishing, will yield and bare his carotid artery to the stronger one. This is an instinctive demonstration of submission that takes place when the weaker wolf knows the other is about to attack. Regardless of whether the spilled blood is still warm, or that his fangs haven't been able to assimilate, there will be no further retaliation that night. The victor will let him go, blocking an impulsive or prepotent response in favor of more appropriate behavior for the pack's survival. Ethologists refer to this phenomenon as "inhibitory control": a key genetic component that entails blocking an impulsive response in favor of a more appropriate alternative when it is advantageous, avoiding that animals of a single species extinguish their species when there are better alternatives: rabbits, dear . . ."

I was watching the television when Zé Antunes showed up.

"You're late," he said.

I guess Bautista said something to him last night, because he didn't give me too much of a hard time. He even showed a little compassion. "You look like shit, Toninho. You must have stayed up late."

Truth is I couldn't complain. I found my way back through the lowlands of Tijuca, I showered in the warehouse, and now I was trying to recover some energy snoozing on the couch during my few minutes of free time. Even when I thought back to the good memories of the previous night, Julia Oliveira's sweet caresses, my head didn't stop throbbing. The hangover was getting worse, turning into a merciless stinger. Standing in front of the television screens, I watched the luminous ballet, the perfect synchronicity of images.

I heard as Zé Antunes greeted the staff, Roberto, Célia, Clarice, Zacarías.

They walked in a line, one after the other, farther into the distance.

"Imagine that we repeatedly roll the same ping pong ball before a group of recently hatched ducklings. Without realizing it, surreptitiously, we may have fixed the process of imprinting that will associate that rolling movement with the identity of the mother, and from then on, it wouldn't be strange to see five little ducklings following behind the ball as they would an adult duck, imitating the same reaction before any sphere that instinctively awakens the need for protection, or running and getting squashed by an irresponsible driver speeding down the road in a car . . ."

Already lulled into snoozing by the whispering voice of the television, Julia was driving her blue sports car and I was by her side, peering out the window at the long thread of highway, the light poles and broad, dark fields, as if everything formed one single, contiguous unit. But mostly I looked at her. I looked at the reflection of her blue profile. The beauty mark on her throat, just beside the jugular. Every once in a while she turned to look at me and her eyes were full of a firm promise that was out of my reach.

Perhaps that's what made me smile: because I felt insecure when she looked at me.

"Humans alone hunt for sport or leisure. All other animals do it for fear of being devoured, or because they are hungry or out competing for territory. If we believe in evolutionary hierarchies, we must accept that human aggressiveness, which has developed to extraordinary levels, has almost perfected the art of cruelty, and that culture has no power over our instincts when confronted by territorial threats or fear of what is different."

Julia smiled as she lay naked on the bed.

"Why do you talk so much about things I don't understand, Toninho?"

I quit going on about the television sets that often seem more expensive than what they are, about pigeons, about serpents.

"You're nuts," she said.

I felt as though my role had been suspended, that the morning breath and hangover that was just waking up might be closer to who I really was.

"You're so beautiful you make me nervous," Toni said.

"Oh, you're such a sweetheart, *tontinho*."

I gazed again at her profile in the glass.

This time her long hair flowed in perfect waves over a green field, gleaming ever more brightly in the light that snuck in through the sliding door. Its slow ascent brought with it the sounds of the mall like morning twitter. A few seconds later, my eyelids opened heavily to a line of ducklings toddling behind a ball on the grass.

"Can I come pick you up later?" I heard.

I looked at Zé Antunes, his hands on his hips, disturbing my line of sight to the television.

"It's time, kid."

I nodded.

But I snuck out without answering, when she was in the shower.

We opened the store around ten. I was only able to rest fifteen minutes. Far from what I would have expected, people flowed by outside with disturbing constancy: an infinite ribbon of heads, urgent strides, and unmet needs. It was life in motion. I had figured a way to be in costume before heading out to my corner in front of the main entrance; the colossal belly covered in green dots; the huge head on top of the small human head; the snout with its two squishy fangs, the pair of well camouflaged holes that allowed me to see. I was once again the bit crocodile promoting the appliances in the Almacenes Mattos, dancing for the children. Making use of my talent, it wasn't long before I attracted the little ones and their parents. With my long legs and strong, agile arms I brought them to the Draco refrigerator section, where Roberto's acumen did the rest. I went back to my corner and kept on dancing. I didn't stop for a moment. Half an hour later, I saw a couple on their way out, followed by Zacarías who was carrying a huge 21-inch screen television set and a coffee maker as gift for the purchase. The couple smiled at each other, clutching each other's hand.

"Toninho," Bautista smiled glowingly.

He was carrying a catalogue of Draco products in his hand, open wide and splendid. The new collection of washers and dryers was arriving soon, a real technological advance that would revolutionize the generic brand market throughout the continent.

"And we'll have them here, in our store," he said, brandishing the pamphlet, giving it little kisses and lightly flicking at it, as if it were a little glass vial and he were about to stick me in the ass with a needle.

"Toni." He slapped me on the back.

As usual, he had a perfect smile.

One of the advantages of my profession is that I can discreetly survey all the people who come in and out of the store. I can make obscene gestures on the sly, stare at cleavage unnoticed. So when I saw Julia approach, alone among the crowd, I wasn't really all that surprised. I was perplexed, scared, but protected in the end under this barrier of cotton and foam that kept me hidden. I watched as she came up the escalator, a magnificent vision parting the multitude. Julia, so radiant, her face lit up by the vitality that good sex imbues on women, walked right by me without even a glance. I knew she'd come all the way from Tijuca just to find me.

"Julia Oliveira," I heard her say to Bautista.

I turned around alarmed, since absentmindedly, I somehow hadn't imagined the possibility of them actually running into each other. But that's just what happened.

"What a surprise to see you in our humble family business," he continued.

Dressed in a provocative décolletage, Julia had made

herself up to survive the light of day better than all the women I had ever known put together. I noted her very light, natural makeup, Julia herself defiant and dignified as she faced the Casanova who didn't deserve her. I felt as though all my sense of security under the head of the foam was starting to melt away, see how she faced him off with courage that I would never have recognized in myself.

"And so?" Julia said, with an even tone of voice. "Do you know where I might find him?"

"Toni?" Bautista laughed.

I felt a shudder going down my long crocodile tail.

"Yes, Toni," she said. "Toninho. Your cousin. Where is he?"

Bautista found my eyes among the crowd.

"He must be at the yacht club in Urca." There was a slight tone of irritation in his voice. "Like any real carioca, he likes to fight against the waves."

My soul found its way back to the crocodile. We were on hand again.

"I'll go look for him in Urca then," Julia said. "*Ciao*, Bautista."

Then she walked by me, elegantly avoiding running into me, a brisk stride.

I didn't exist for her anymore.

I did nothing to avoid it. I didn't say a word as she

walked away. I let the two holes in my costume point too directly at her magnificent backside as she sank down the escalator and the first floor wasted no time in swallowing her whole.

A little later, Bautista went after her. I could tell he was truly furious with me, though by no means did he let it show or did I wish to interpret him that way. Things were good the way they were. It wasn't worth ruining the day. When he walked by me he whispered that I owed him an explanation, and I think he said it more for not having stayed Toni all night long than for having fucked his girlfriend five or six times.

I kept dancing, twirling, and dancing some more until Gal Costa showed up to relieve me.

So I stopped the kids who were cavorting all around me and walked back to the store without allowing anyone or anything to get in my way, immune to all pleas and appeals. Even still, one of the kids found a way to hang on to my tail, but I brushed the little devil off and he ended up near the washing machines. I continued on fearlessly, ignoring the scolding words that Zé, Bautista or any other client might have, parents of conservative families trying to teach their children proper manners. Surprisingly, nobody came after me. Nobody dared say a word to me. The only person I came across on my way was Célia, the cellular technology salesperson who tried to cheer me up with the same hollow smile she offered everyone.

"Just tell them whatever, I had to go to the bathroom."

"I'll cover for you," she said, "but don't expect me to for more than five minutes."

I thought she was going to add "or I'll come and look for you," but the door swung shut and interrupted my musing.

In any case, I was feeling annoyed.

Once inside I didn't go directly to the bathroom as I'd said; first I took the enormous head off and left it by the faucet. All I really wanted was to be able to take the other one off, too, that soft spiral that sunk to nowhere inside of my body.

I walked to the stall and searched around in my pants pockets till I came across a little sky blue envelope I had bought a few hours earlier on the road to Tijuca. I took the pill out, dropped it in a glass of water and waited, watching how it disintegrated into a thousand milky bubbles on the surface. I watched it drop like a shipwreck taken down by gravity, thinning out till the final convulsion when it completely disintegrated. I thought about the lobsters reproducing in direct proportion to good sales. In Célia smiling at me with something more than kindness before disappearing. In Julia looking for me in all the yachts docked in Urca. In Bautista so proud of having the full Draco catalogue long before any other store in the mall. I even thought about Daniela Mercury. In the wolves that are pigeons and the pigeons that are wolves. In animals that let you off the hook. Maybe my throat had been bared a long time before I knew I was going to lose. Or maybe I could roll my own ping pong balls at life and get someone to follow me, at least for a few meters, for whatever was left of it.

As I watched the glass, I thought I'd found the answer to many of life's mysteries, but lacked the words to share them with the world. It didn't really matter. It was all about me and this moment in time. Vigorously, and inspired by a strange sense of dignity, I listened to a whining kid complain, his father's indignant outcry, and maybe then my name pronounced through the partition walls of the warehouse. I heard footsteps of someone coming to look for me, threatening, and, finally still, the headache that came apart in thousands of adrenaline-filled bubbles, I put the crocodile's head back on and waited for them standing on my two feet, ready to give them hell.

My name is Antonio Carlos Pereira. Toninho.

I was ready.

Lessons for a Child
Who Arrives Late

WE COULD SENSE that a shadow had stroked the door, but it couldn't have been the cat. My sister Candelaria was the first to notice it. She stopped playing the piano at nearly the same time. Drowsy from the lesson's stammering repetition, I surveyed a colossal painting that hung in the salon, of a nude woman reclining beside a grotto, scarcely veiled by the modesty of her hair, one of her hands fallen to her side, like a leaf. I couldn't be bothered to try to figure out why the apple in her hand should weigh so heavily as to tire her forearm that way. What's more, Miss Chevalier's eyes were wide open, and with them she followed the score of a sonata my sister was now playing too hesitantly. So it was nearly impossible that the intruder, who had already succeeded in disturbing the C Major keys beneath my sister's fingers, could sink further into the piano's wood while going unnoticed. Or that the teacher, who by now had turned her head to scrutinize the open door, wouldn't move somehow to correct the breach of courtesy that she would never have excused of us.

"Pardon the interruption, children," she said ceremoniously.

She stood up and we watched as she disappeared along the path previously reconnoitered by her eyes.

Margarita walked in, held at the arm by Miss Chevalier, and came to a standstill in the middle of the salon, eyes lowered and brows raised, smoothing crisply and kittenishly a pleat in her little dress. My sister continued angrily striking one of the keys; and the sight of the girl brought to mind those crumpled papers left strewn across the floor after a party, with little toys and pieces of candy spilled from the abdomen of a clubbed piñata. Margarita curtsied, clutching the lace of her salmon-colored dress and seeming to age a little in the exercise, in the time it took to gather her skirts, bend her knees, straighten herself back up, and pinch a rather poor imitation of an adult woman's pouty frown, as if her derision in some way served as a tonic for having to enact the ceremony at all, and in this little rebellious act, this lack of domestication in her face, she could somehow salvage herself from a compulsory humiliation. The piano note, played over and over like a hammer, finally digressed. At that precise moment, Margarita spoke her name, and Miss Chevalier, now appeased by the discreet and modest intonation with which that name had been pronounced, let her go.

"A young lady must never draw inappropriate attention to herself," Miss Chevalier said as she took her seat and arranged with both hands, the mauve-hued linen skirts she always wore when giving lessons. "Either she's noticed for what she is or better not noticed at all."

Obviously her niece—I found out later that's who she was—couldn't have cared less about the lesson in decorum or being forced to enact the theatricals of politesse. The second the old woman's attention was diverted, Margarita signaled me over to the yard outside and I shrugged in response to say that I wasn't sure whether to follow or stay.

The elderly woman caught sight of our hurried negotiation and agreed that our going outdoors would be the best thing for the afternoon. She settled her spectacles onto her nose—a long and emphatic nose down which nothing dared slip—and stiffly now, her attention once again fixed on the piano, told us we were both excused.

"I want to see you back here in forty minutes, Gregorio," she scolded me before the fact; and glimpsing the envy in my little sister's eyes, added, pointing straight at her: "You had better get started."

2.

The Chevalier residence's yard was, more than anything else, a great esplanade of unruly grass in which shocks of weeds sprouting here and there interrupted puddles of dry dirt. Despite all efforts to stop them, the weeds propagated with the incontinence of an ancient hunger. There were mostly shrubs along the brinks and leafy bushes that provided shade even when the sun wasn't out. They formed small cays of thick vegetation where Margarita and I eventually found refuge, particularly in the shade of an almond tree, whose pink leaves could be seen from the town's main street in the springtime, a massive and incongruous tree that was nothing short of a miracle, since everything in its environs was like a wasteland. The community's educated men had the custom of tipping their hats at the tree, wiping the sweat from their brow, and the gesture of its blooming always filled the women with romantic longing, or melancholy.

For some reason, Margarita wanted first to test my devotion, perhaps the exertion of our introduction had put her in a foul mood, or perhaps because she had finally found a playmate to redeem the boredom of every day. I saw her look at me askance, goading me to approach her in the far corner of the garden.

"Ah, you want me to dig," I said, pointing to the shovel sticking out from a pile of freshly picked weeds and broken ground.

Margarita didn't answer; but I knew that yes, that was exactly what she wanted, for me to excavate. I didn't think a plastic shovel would serve against that hard earth, but I gave it a try anyway. I was stirred by a desire to please her, so I began turning the soil.

Before long, she took the shovel away from me. She was older than me, so she had no difficulty in removing a stiff, crusty scab of earth, which came up with an ill-fated clump of roots filched from the grass.

It wasn't until I observed the ground bitten by the void that I finally understood what she was after: a few cochineal bugs spilled out, scampering to hide themselves again, like modest women trying to conceal their bodies. Other ones, maybe older and more audacious, coiled up like accordions exhaling the sound of their own resignation.

I looked up and she grinned, pointing at that quiet ruckus; I watched her take out an empty marmalade jar and drop the little bugs inside that she'd caught with her fingers.

I was expecting her to say something, to scold me for showing disgust when I picked them up, but she just went back to digging, a smile taking over her face as she snatched them up again, far from caring at all about me.

It allowed me to observe her more closely.

The first thing I noticed about her was the functional armistice struck by her little black shoes against the coarseness of the crabgrass. They were finished in patent leather and had the luster of an apple skin that's been polished on the sleeve of a jacket. The only thing new about them was the shine; the leather itself was cracked, and despite the detailing, they showed the signs of wear and tear.

What's more, Margarita was petite like her aunt, and so fair that her veins showed unnaturally through the skin of her arms, even though they were plump and soft like the rest of her body. It was as if there was a woven network of little worms beneath her skin, a strange fluvial cartography that got tangled up in its own sinuous curves and slopes. Her legs gave several indications of being robust yet supple, and were sheathed in smoke-colored tights; and she wore her terrifically long, tangled hair down in a sort of wild aureole. When she smiled, her teeth would sit like a sharp little row of fangs along a wrinkled band of red gums. No matter how often she smiled, or under what circumstances, the sight always frightened me, though I tried not to let it show. How many times did I avoid making a joke so as not to see her happy! If she wrote down a comment that obliged me to laugh, I'd restrain myself. I'd leave her bewildered or gloomy, but her smile to me was like a dangerous precipice.

It was from this edge precisely that I watched her smiling: plucking up cochineals and filling a glass jar with them, tumbling to the bottom, upside down, the concert of their quick, unproductive little legs.

After a while, we got bored with the cochineal routine and the space in the garden where they could be found, and went to dig up other areas of earth, excavating new ground or contemplating the tiny universe hidden beneath the leaf of a tree. Margarita's eyes lit up with each minute creature she rustled up. She'd watch them move, a little worm arching its long, spongy body: a snail stiffening its antennae, and she'd let out an eager squeal that I always mistook for panic when it was in fact pure joy.

That afternoon I remarked, just to make conversation:

"Imagine how many insects we could dig up if our shovel wasn't made of plastic."

She never responded, perhaps out of shyness or some other misgiving, just placed the shovel in my hands before vanishing back into the house. I saw her walk away in prolonged strides, as if her hips were somehow weighing her down; and then I saw was myself imitating her harsh stabs at the earth, this time by the edge of a brick wall that shed pinkish dust when my shovel sunk down and burrowed. I found nothing we hadn't seen before: snails, worms, cochineals . . . (ants were apparently of no interest to her and I thought I could understand why); I must have told her, somewhat embarrassed, that I hadn't come across anything new when she gathered the pleats of her dress and sat down by my side.

"I'm sorry," I said, giving her back the shovel.

We shared a few more mysteries, rooting among the leaves and covering ourselves in the clammy earth we molded with our hands. But it was true: no new bugs, and after a while we gave up grubbing around in the tree bark, in the orifices of the walls, or under a brick that had settled itself firmly into the mud.

At some point, Margarita opened the kit she had brought along concealed in her dress, and once again, I caught a glimpse of those little teeth that seemed to suffer in laughter.

"Tweezers?" I asked, looking at what she fetched, worried that now she wanted to play at some cosmetic enterprise typical of *mademoiselles*.

One by one we extracted the instruments from the case, the tweezers, a nail clipper, files, and a small pair of curvy, blunt-edged nostril-hair scissors. We observed them solemnly, as children do the most everyday, innocuous objects. I sensed a slight, excited twitch in her arm and though I didn't hear her say so, I knew she was inviting me to share in what had triggered her little shiver; I turned around just in time to see a cricket cautiously recoiling, closing its useless wings, unable to hop, intimidated perhaps by the peculiar shadow by which Margarita and I both held it motionless along the edge. We never gave it time to adjust its flight instinct. I leveled the vessel she'd reserved for the bigger insects, and the cricket landed smack in the cardboard box on its first hop, looking at us almost sorrowfully and bereft of any desire to jump again. Margarita surveyed the instruments we'd taken from her aunt's kit, then stared me straight in the eyes, seeking absolution there that she wasn't able to give herself. Yet there was also an expression of glee in her eyes, their long lashes opening and closing as if clapping mischievously.

I understood what she wanted, and said yes.

She began cutting the cricket's antennae off with the little scissors, which kept it still and disoriented. It was easy for us to stretch its body out with the tweezers once it was no longer able to jump, the bigger legs first, then the six little ones. If we'd had a magnifying glass, we could've seen how much it resembled a frog.

But we didn't.

It was just a cricket cut to pieces.

3.

I hated when Margarita cracked her knuckles when it was her turn to play the piano. She knew how the sound she made when she laced her fingers together and twisted them, like cracking walnuts, triggered a slight nervous twitch I wasn't able to conceal. But she didn't crack her joints like that, like crushing snail shells underfoot, only to annoy me; in fact, it was her reminder of how much happier we both were outdoors and not below that roof.

But to preserve the serene cycle of things, Margarita and I had to play the piano when Miss Chevalier told us to. Really, I was the one who had to play. My mother dropped Candelaria and me off at around four in the afternoon, and would come to fetch us two hours later, rushing to make it home in time to cook dinner for Papá. That's why I always let Candelaria go first, so I could run out and play in the garden with Margarita. Later, I would scrub my hands and obey the old woman's instructions; simple scales to start, now a fugue so that my growing fingers "would search out the sound in their bones." I was seven years old at the time and Margarita was nine, but she had started much earlier since her father was a pianist; so every time Miss Chevalier wanted to encourage my sister and me, she asked Margarita to play for us. In the meantime, my sister would sneak out to play with the cat, until she finally got bored with its indifference and came back to sit in a chair next to me. That's when the old woman would tell us to be still now, not a single sound, and take her place beside her niece. Seeing Margarita's fingers traipsing about the keys, her fingernails chewed to the nib and outlined with earth, Miss Chevalier would let out a sigh that sounded more like the emanation of her soul, and tilt her head sideways.

"Bach," she'd say. "Concerto in F minor. *Allegro*."

And even though her little shoes didn't reach the floor, Margarita would start to play, as if the words uttered by the old woman were some secret code only they could decipher, and now engaged to illuminate the world.

"*Vité*," she said again, in code.

Each time it took a little under nine minutes to finish the piece.

But I felt immersed in time watching the dizzying leaps of her fingers, which were like raindrops plunking against the hard earth, and it always seemed to last longer. I would close my eyes and there she was out in the yard again, spinning around and around on an invisible axis centered on her heels and her little salmon-colored dress, and her pale, plump arms held tight to her torso. The fingers playing the keys, devoid of any other authority beyond her own desire, and the folds of that delicate fabric lifting like a horseless carousel, and a cascade of black-

and-white, tense, and unconstrained keys rained down, as if there before my eyes, the opening of the swirling little dress, the hands and the body, became the umbrella that sheltered us from a world that could never drench us again.

To me, these were the lessons given to a child who always arrived late. The crippled boy, who followed the sound of the flute hobblingly, clumsily, unable to catch its rhythm, its controlled movement, or ascertain the proper strength with which to strike each key. But how I enjoyed listening to it, like when it rained and the particles of a cloudburst would play on the leaves and the branches and the earth that concealed us. Margarita played piano with a sort of despotic unconcern, as if the world had gone deaf and the only sound that remained was a voice trapped in its own chords. As if unspoken words were vibrating there, and that spasm, in that shiver of not wanting to speak, they resisted the urge to release sound; to avoid falling into my ears they clung to the wood with both hands.

And Miss Chevalier was aware of it, too; there was something sorrowful in the way she let her hand fall upon her cheek when she listened to her niece playing; something that made me consider how difficult it was to cultivate a talent being lost like the climax at the end of a concert; as if the form of sound that each tap of Margarita's fingers captured and then set free, only corroborated a flight instinct that was impossible to curtail. Like a butterfly without the window, fluttering its wings in the wind as they disintegrate in mid-air.

Though Miss Chevalier loved the music, they both knew she would never be able to catch it.

We saw her expression turn firm again in the languorous green of her eyes when they opened, which always ended in the phrase:

"You'll never be like Gould."

But that was an opinion, like so many others.

4.

The third time we saw each other, Margarita had already harvested all sorts of insects in shoeboxes and glass jars, a nervous collection we hid in the roots of the almond tree in case Miss Chevalier should at any point invade our sanctuary. That way, we could take them out whenever we needed to put their springiness to the test, or their resistance to fire or salt or some other liquid or corrosive material that occurred to us, to see how many different ways, tidy or otherwise, we could make them stay still. At times we would contrive quick trials in which a snail naturally had to be punished for being so slow. Or a moth, for eating a piece of Margarita's dress. Or a stray bee for trying to sting us, vengefully, as it buzzed around the inside of a plastic container. Being cruel to the insects never made me feel sadness or remorse, though the perverse and ingenious inventory of activities that a small and sweet child like Margarita was able to improvise never ceased to amaze me. We started classifying the insects according to their ability to resist pain, maybe because they were so tiny and silent. I guess it was rather like pulling some body's eyelashes off. At that age, it wasn't a degree of pain high enough to impress us, and in hindsight, I don't think it ever has. It was as if the insects' bodies weren't real: at most they were mere accidents, segments, extensions of earth pulled from the earth. And little more. They were often far away; they'd get lost and end up like an invisible simulacrum of life. Whenever something went wrong, what we felt was akin to disgust, I mean, something akin to pain; little more than a shiver up the spine: grub squished by accident prompted a curled nostril; a snail emptied of its viscous liquid, under the scab of its extirpated shell, barely incited a minor squeamishness.

None of it ever seemed strange to me. After all, she was the first girl I'd ever known who wasn't a relative of mine. And a girl could be however she wanted, even cruel.

The only person I ever told about my garden escapades was Marino, a schoolmate who had a perpetual piece of snot clogging one of his nostrils. I ran into him one morning in the market when my mother was selecting a chicken whose neck had been slit and bled out, and they were plucking the feathers after having scalded it in boiling water a moment earlier. Marino went on and on about his recent trip into the city, where his father's family had an apartment looking over the sea; oh, how fun, I told him, but there was no comparison with what Margarita and I had been up to in Miss Chevalier's yard, and I spilled the details. Afterward, Marino stared at me pensively, wiped his brow and retorted categorically:

"Must be because she's deaf."

I wasn't quite old enough yet to fully grasp a notion like the absence of sound, much less the kind of distance that a handicap can occasion between people; but acting out on his revelation, I submerged myself one night in the still water of the bathtub and lingered there a long time, an interminable minute, struggling to understand what Margarita's world must feel like, a world without sound, and sound without a world. I began thrashing around and rescued my head from the bathwater. Once back in the real world, I felt I could breathe again, the world had swelled anew, but I was now hearing everything differently.

The following day, Margarita didn't point me toward the yard, as was her custom. She must have sensed something peculiar straightaway, I could tell she was acting differently toward me and she wanted me to know as much. There was a new inquisitiveness in my gaze, perhaps in excess, which must have tipped her off to the fact that I now knew what it was she had never wished to tell me herself.

That day she took out a little magnetic board that wiped itself clean every time she pulled a panel at the bottom. That's how she started writing to me, partly by accident, and partly because I had obliged her to it. We carried the board outside with us, together with the instruments of torture, and every time she wanted something she would write it out on the top panel with a lead-tip pencil. This awkward handwriting obliged my eyes to replicate the sounds as she wrote them down and thereby imitate her voice. I don't know whether it was on account of our games. By end of the third week, I had settled into a singular way of listening to her, and it seemed as though her crooked letters, which appeared to sink down into ribbons of mercury, could permeate my ears by way of my eyes, taking on whimsical meanings that slanted as she wrote them out, each one of the letters tilting like a new tonality, a tiny symptom of her voice infiltrating my body.

I remember as if it were yesterday the first thing she said about my method:

"Gregory, you are a perfect fool."

Then she wrote:

"I don't ever want to see you again, not even if you bring me your mother's waxing kit."

But she saw me again. I fetched her my mother's waxing kit and we spent the rest of the summer playing with one of her favorite materials in the art of insect torture: hair removal wax. It worked like this: first we heated the wax in a small aluminum recipient. Once it became a boiling liquid, we harvested it very carefully and then smothered any body we found in the yard with the stuff. That's how we built a miniature wax museum collection, with all kinds of tiny fauna. Margarita continued perfecting the process, demonstrating a true talent for arrested movement. She would smear the bug just enough for it to keep moving forward, and we would watch as it progressively slowed down till it stood perfectly calm, fighting the friction of the wax before turning into a statue.

It's amazing the things that can amuse children at that age. It's all we needed to keep us entertained. And we were happy.

5.

The day the farming truck crushed Papá's car, the hunting had been bountiful; the marmalade jar had stirred into a roiling mass, the tight body of an earthworm colony. We trapped at least fifty of them, but despite our early bonanza I had to give it up because my mother obliged me to stay home for two days to help her clean out my father's room. I struggled with boxes heaped with clothes and documents that smelled of my family's already old story. We'd had no time to put his things in order, and neither did he, but within the natural order of our still life together he seemed to have gone in peace, and us along with him. He'd been so taciturn and detached over the past few years, it took us a while to realize he was gone, maybe he'd already died a long time ago.

The following day I accompanied my mother, my grandmother, and my great grandmother in the funeral

cortege, all three of them dressed in black like me, walking until the weight of the coffin sapped the strength of
the six Indians who were carrying it on their shoulders in
front of us. I watched the men wipe the sweat from their
faces with stiff, faded rags that were quickly and care-
lessly stuffed back into their pants, the edges left dangling
from their pockets like tongues voicing the fatigue they
weren't allowed to express themselves. The cemetery
soil had already been exhumed and piled into a mound
at the end of the street; a damp alcove was there waiting for my father, and beside it stood the priest, smoking
his last cigarette of the afternoon, impatient to be on his
way. He was a friend of my grandmother's, according to
her. We watched him raise his hand and flick the butt to
the ground, murmuring a few worn-out words of condo-
lence, as if he were throwing them into the hole too, just
a few more ashes to step on. He took out his purple stole
and kissed it before hanging it around his neck. Once
his ceremonial dress was complete, he improvised a few
quick words, skipping the habitual complacent obituar-
ies and fervent remembrances. My mother didn't even
take out a handkerchief, or moisten her eyes along with
the others, a custom among young widows who planned
on rebuilding their lives, considering this the moment to
get started. The grandmothers moved their heads as if
the warning had come late; and the few friends of my
father's in attendance seemed to have trouble recogniz-

ing his portrayal given the weight of his fleeting passage through this world.

"And Jesus said: 'I am the resurrection, and the life: he that believeth in me, though he were dead, yet shall he live: And whosoever liveth and believeth in me shall never die . . .'"

It was my place to throw the first handful of earth into the open pit, into whose darkness the casket had descended. I clenched the clump of damp earth in my fist and for some reason, perhaps it was the grainy, inert feel of the soil that affected me so, I couldn't choke back the tears, or hold the resistance that my swollen face had promised not to surrender. As I struggled, that little chunk of the world began to sprinkle in the direction it was meant to, sinking in the way it was meant to because we all fall down in the end, and the muffled sound of the earth striking that wooden lid, so much like the sound of my father drumming the tabletop with his fingers, made me break into sobs; because Lazarus, who had been four days dead and rose to his feet when Jesus Christ called out to him, hands and feet bound with bandages, and He said, heedless of the commotion his miracle had brought, "loose him and let him go."

"And raising his eyes to the heavens, Jesus said, 'Father, I thank thee that thou hast heard me.'"

In the end, all those gathered there followed the same

ritual: wept a little and scattered a bit of earth over the wooden lid.

I thought about how weary my father's hands would have been after drumming his fingers on the table for so long, how his age-old gesture of impatience, so familiar, had nearly been absolved by the distance that softens memory, because now he had nothing left to play, now there was only silence, except for the priest's voice using up the last of the gospel, and the crisp sound of the six Indians' shovels digging into the earth and filling the hole to the brim, to the level of our feet.

In the distance I saw my grandmother tug a handkerchief from her cleavage, revealing a few bills and several coins hidden in its folds, whose austere shine seemed to express gratitude at having been set free. She placed them in the palms of the six Indians' hands, who acknowledged her silently before returning to their places on a bench.

By the time the hole was properly filled, the only person left was Miss Chevalier, who may have arrived late, and who approached us wishing to speak to my mother and me.

"It will be difficult for him to continue his lessons," my mother said at some point, without looking at me.

"I understand," the old woman answered.

"Now that his father is gone, things will be a little difficult, you see?"

Miss Chevalier understood again.

"It's a lot of money," my mother emphasized, and I saw how she felt more comfortable by being insistent. "By the end of the summer, I may be forced to listen to my mother and return with her to San Miguel."

The old woman reassured her:

"Summer is nearly over."

"Yes," my mother said, relieved to find another justification that wasn't due to her condition of being a young widow.

And yet, beneath the soft black wool I felt the bones of her hand clutch mine, and I couldn't say if she was squeezing it to protect or hurt me. I pulled my hand away and she overcame her anxiety quickly, embarrassed; and I watched her go over to grandmother, who was still whispering something to the priest.

"I'm so sorry," Miss Chevalier said addressing me now. "How are you feeling?"

I didn't know what to feel.

"That's normal—at your age you can hardly fathom what life is yet. Let alone death."

But I already knew plenty about death. I knew it was like a snail squished against the ground. Or an earthworm stuck to the sole of a shoe. Or a cricket cut into little pieces, or a cochineal wrinkling itself up into a ball. What I didn't know was how to live stuck inside the crude, roughhewn wood of a boy who was trying to become a man.

Mamá gestured to me furtively from her place by my grandmother, and I asked the old woman if I could call on Margarita, knowing that it was unlikely I would see her again that afternoon.

"Of course," she said. "Come whenever you'd like."

So I extended my hand to her, and she shook it with interest, as if she were picking a leaf up off the ground.

"What a shame," she said before letting go. "You have the fingers of a pianist."

6.

"How lucky," Margarita wrote.

We saw no sign of movement through the glass marmalade jar, and figured the earthworms must have died since they'd spent three days and three nights tangled in a ball in our hiding place, unable to breathe. I thought it was better that way, but when she screwed the lid off, we caught the aroma of moist earth. I watched what looked like a twisting nerve squirm back into the tangle, and in no time it had aroused a synchronized chaos of bodies that began writhing in a thick, muddy sludge.

Margarita pulled out a cluster of worms and let them wriggle in the palm of her left hand. A few of them twisted fully around, as if they were reawakening, and I thought I could distinguish the whimsy of letters in their mindless coils, as if they were trying to tell me something in their own peculiar way. We watched them for a while under the sun.

"What do you mean how fortunate?" I said.

"That your dad died," she wrote again. "You're so lucky."

Papá hadn't always been such a mean type, in fact every once in a while, when he wasn't beating my mother, he could even seem pleasant. Truth is he spent too much time away from home for me to ever properly hate him. Whenever I fell quiet during dinner, at a loss for words, he would start drumming his fingers on the table waiting for his meal to be served; it happened a lot, since I never really had much to say to him. Regardless, I didn't think my father deserved to die that way; really nobody deserved to die.

"Mine did," Margarita wrote.

That's when I remembered.

It happened the afternoon we caught a scorpion. A black one that threatened several times with the stinger at the tip of its long tail, though all it really seemed to want was to be left alone. I didn't dare try to catch it with the plastic scoop, but she told me it was crucial: if we succeeded, we could slip it in an envelope and send it by mail to her father, who lived far away, on the other side of the ocean.

Her little round face lit up, but I was very tactful:

"That's silly," I said. "It would be long dead by the time they delivered it to his house."

Margarita looked crestfallen.

"If I could," she wrote, "I'd cut each one of his fingers off with a little pair of scissors so he'd never be able to play the piano again."

We hadn't seen each other for over a week.

The afternoon seemed endless now, without the lessons, and it reminded me of the days in San Miguel; a single, lingering, sticky afternoon over which no night ever falls.

"I won't be coming anymore," I said, recalling the conversation between my mother and Miss Chevalier in the cemetery, and the knot in my throat caused my voice to break.

"I know," she had written.

"How did you know?"

"Because everyone leaves eventually," she wrote again.

Over the next six days, without her aunt controlling her every move, without having to practice the piano as a digression for her fingers, Margarita dug a hole near the almond tree big enough to fit her, and eventually to fit both of us, with nothing more than the plastic scoop. I could imagine the patience it took as I surveyed the long burrow that peeked out from the underbrush in our little corner of the yard. She signaled it without grandstanding. I simply followed her gaze down to her little patent leather shoes that weren't very shiny anymore, like a pair of melancholy hedgehogs.

I drew closer to the dark edge; there was a naked shock of almond tree roots springing from the walls. I couldn't see anything more than the clefts in the hollowed space, like parched gums in a hungry mouth. I sensed the faint, delicate fragrance of grass, like after a hard rain when the whole world seems to have brought everything to an end, but you bring your nose to the ground and sniff, and realize that in fact everything is just beginning.

"So what are you going to do now?" I asked, turning towards her and pointing to the tunnel that already separated my world from hers.

She must have expected my response, because before I was fully turned to her, she had already written:

"I think you already know."

She seemed to hesitate for a moment, as I did; but at last her letters invited me in with her. And I didn't waver; I was thrilled to be included.

"You go first," she wrote.

She handed me the plastic scoop she'd used all by herself.

"In case you get to the end," she wrote.

I brushed the branches of the almond tree out of the way and got down to crawl, feeling the soft, damp heaviness of the earth on my knees. We set her little writing board down by the rim. She handed me a flashlight. And I entered as deeply as I could, because surely there were insects here that nobody had ever seen before, or squished between their fingers, and I wanted to be the first to find them and squish them between my fingers. But this was Margarita's world more than it was mine and I realized

that: it was silent and aromatic, full of textures and re-
liefs. And darkness. I knew that because my head had
already started molding to the confines when I touched
the dry outer edge of that burrow, but my body felt some
natural panic and tried to pull itself back, for fear it might
never be able to return. My knees pulled me backwards.
I screamed her name three or four times, sobbing, until I
realized she couldn't hear me: I may be inside her world
now, but nothing had changed on the outside. I understood all of this. I held the flashlight in my hand and it
shone a weary, yellow oval whose shape changed and dis-
torted whenever it projected against the walls. The only
thing I could see in the light was the thirsty throat of the
earth, all sediment and roots, like the bearded strings of
a broken puppet. I took a breath, made sure I was still
breathing, and realized my only alternative was to push
on, so I thrust out my arm that was holding the plastic
scoop and began burrowing into the dirt with such ease
that I was surprised a girl older than me hadn't gone any
further than this.

Piles of dirt accumulated along the sides of my tunnel,
and I forced myself to pass straight through its center,
burrowing my way in, when I heard a voice that sounded
like newly dampened soil:

"I told you it would work."

But I was moving forward with too much hunger and
couldn't stop to hear a new voice. All I did was pile earth
on either side, and we sank.

Madureira Knows

FARINELLI WAILED again for hours that night. He'd started up ever since the neighbors began taking their black bags outside when the lower ranks of the police force went on strike, and the bags amassed on our outer shores like unclaimed bodies in a morgue. When the accumulation took on the consistency of a wall, elevated and a little gooey from the heat, the chatter among some of the neighbors included moving the bags of waste ten or fifteen kilometers southward, to save ourselves from the stench and the infection carried in their miasmas. But the idea never prospered, it was stillborn.

We realized two weeks later that our neighborhood unit council only served to delay the project, but by then we had already grown accustomed to the smell that crept its way up the nine floors of our building. Saddled with that, it wasn't long before we also got used to Farinelli's nocturnal visits, his rotten wailing that accompanied us the rest of summer. His was a prolonged, shrill moan that stretched on and on like a rubber band and once he got started, it kept me awake for hours. I heard it despite the concrete slab walls and the fifteen meters that separated us from the ground floor.

It wasn't long before I decided to tell Valdemar about it during one of our lesson. The previous night's scene was still fresh in my mind, how after leaving a few black bags next to the dumpster, I wandered around under the star-studded January sky. The image still throbbed hot in my head, and it kept going round and round until I could finally transform it into words. So I told Valdemar about it; I told him everything, and he merely looked back at me with that austere, self-sufficient pout that I came to detest.

"You mean Farinelli," he said.

But he didn't understand. "It's not a boy who wails, Valdemar. It's a cat . . . a cat that lives with us on the block somewhere."

I don't know why, but I breathed uneasily when I finished talking, as if I had gone back downstairs again, as if I were looking straight at it, unmoving between the black mounds surrounding our block's outer fence. I told Valdemar that he was there alright, his supple body, scratching at the bags made opaque by the street lights, sniffing at white viscera recently spilled from plastic containers, wrinkled papers, freed over the gravel. Farinelli moved with a weird, mechanical perfection, smoothing and flattening before he came to a stop. It was as if I could feel him tense and arch his back myself, and maybe that's why, to calm my growing anxiety, I clapped my palms together thinking that if I frightened him, I might somehow cleanse my own fear, too. But Farinelli didn't move. Far from what I expected, his eyes shone confidently and he bared his fangs with viscous, somnolent ferocity.

"Then what?" Valdemar seemed interested.

"He ran off. Out through a hole in the chain link fence," I said.

The old man nodded his head and went on nodding as he placed the trembling needle of his stereo into action for the first time. A nasally voice sounded throughout the room, quivering as though it had scratched a pipe.

"It's not the real Farinelli," he said immediately, "but he's no worse than our little friend."

We listened to the melancholy song for about five minutes, about a man who seemed to travel across time and through the music itself, and then he turned it off.

"Now he's your cat, too," he said. "You can give him any name you want."

But Farinelli was a good name. And it stuck.

I asked him to put that warm, fragile voice back on for me, if only for a little while, and Valdemar nodded again and the old contraption clicked back into motion. I listened until the needle crossed the record's entire radial, until the wobbly pulse of the rings going round the record reached a void where it didn't know how to keep them spinning anymore.

I was eight years old at the time, and lived with my father on the seventh floor of the southern wing of the fifth housing unit on our block. We had moved there five years earlier, after Mamá took off with a lover six years younger than her to live a more spontaneous lifestyle and left without saying goodbye. A few weeks later, my father decided he too wanted to run away from it all, which included the city, and the letter and the telephone number he never thought to share with me. We left the house we were renting in Juiz de Fora without recovering our deposit, and ten hours later we arrived at the apartment he'd never dared to take our family of three, even though he was the proprietor. I vaguely remember the first day we spent there, the city moving upwards now, for the first time, towards the sky; and from on high, the lights were shortened by the powdery reflections at the bottom of the lake, and the buildings moved by the city's uncontainable current, which swelled up along a great range of mountains that were still unbroken.

It didn't take long for me to understand that my father wanted to provide me with an extended family to compensate for his inability to keep Mamá by our side. After all, that's what all the other people who had come to live in our unit were supposed to be; people who came moved by faith, by integrity, or simply because they were desperate, who bought into the official space of the Government's dream. One way or another, they all shared a belief in collective life. But the housing units, despite their dense demographic, remained a solitary place for me. I was never able to participate in the hushed alliances the children formed, or the thoughtful invitations—my standoffishness always got in the way—tendered by women dressed in aprons so different from the ones my mother always wore in my romantic memory of her, which I struggled to hold on to. I kept outside of the social rituals that went on around me, of the daily choices on the tiny stage of my life and my future, without the courage to join the cruel symmetry hidden in the games and the pacts that were made beforehand. I never learned how to kick a ball with precision or dive into the lake like the other kids, or go on my bike beyond a certain safe area, beyond the green commons that surrounded our broad expanse of cement slabs. The bright lights of the new city pierced our movements and under its solitary, sterile glare, I often found myself musing about Mamá, that invisible Mamá still waiting for me with her tender arms open wide, some place we had never shared.

It was a Tuesday afternoon, towards the end of December, when Papá took me to meet Valdemar. It came as a surprise since up until then, outside of the weekly council meetings held in a man-made grotto in the commons, we had only mingled with neighbors when it was convenient, associating as little as possible and with the detached politeness that kept us from becoming too familiar.

Ten minutes later, we were standing in front of a rickety sign that read: "Valdemar Madureira. Professor of Mathematics and Logic." I could hear the sound of a little bell teetering from inside the room, as if we had made a wish and thrown a coin into the depth of a well. I pressed the doorbell again and the inevitable sounds followed: the footsteps and the door's safety bolt sliding. Finally, the handle started to turn. The whole sequence of reactions, I thought, hadn't begun with me pushing that bell, but much earlier in fact; maybe even a few weeks earlier, when Miss Rovênia recounted my failings as if she were diagnosing some incurable disease.

"Professor Madureira," my father greeted him.

The calm expression that accompanied his greeting made me aware that it wasn't the first time they'd met.

"Lucio," he said.

We shook hands and Valdemar invited us in. My father seemed to like the home's austerity, jammed with books and keepsakes still arranged with an unequivocally feminine air. Valdemar offered crackers, which we sampled out of politeness, and we listened as he praised mathematics and the good time we would have together. Whenever he talked, his hands would describe grand gestures in the air; he was the kind of person full of harmless gestures, and when it came down to it he was just another lonely person who, like us, had come in search of a family.

Papá nodded gratefully when they agreed on a price for my lessons, looking at me every once in a while to make sure we had a deal: private lessons four times a week instead of being grounded for a month.

"We're on, right?" Papá said.

I nodded back.

My father stood up finally, and old Valdemar walked us to the door. From inside, we imagined how the brilliant and bustling street would cut like a wound before our eyes. I strained to blink, but through the sudden dazzle I could still locate his open-mouthed smile.

"Till Tuesday," Valdemar said, holding out his pulpy hand that shook mine limply.

I nodded, this time sincerely.

My father gave me five *cruzeiros* to cancel out my summer, and patted me on the head in an armistice worse than being grounded.

Sometimes I liked to walk along the fence, although lately the stench had gotten worse and it tended to encourage me to return home. Papá warned me against walking in that area; some kids had already gotten sick, but I didn't care because unlike the others, I had never come down with the chicken pox or the measles or any of those childhood illnesses that keep you stuck to the sheets for weeks at a time. So each time Papá fell asleep, I would switch off the television and do my house chores—leave the bags near the overfull dumpster—and then walk a while around the landscaped commons that were designed to connect our unit with the next one, 54 South, near the edge of the highway. There was no noise at night, when the block settles into a serene quietude that always made me drowsy. But by the time that happened, I was usually back home and in bed, and it didn't take more than a few minutes for me to fall asleep, peering into the darkness of my room as if I were really staring into the big skies above New City: that solid color overtaken by strange purple tones, which slowly turn into a solid color again, mixed with the pigment of a renewed dream.

I could do it sometimes: see the stars, their brightness and the twinkling lights that transform the night into a different place.

Suddenly I would open my eyes and see the low-hanging firmament; but I was often still outside, among the garbage and the penetrating smells of the dusk.

"Aren't you afraid of walking by yourself in this deserted place?" I heard someone say behind me.

I contained my panicked scream and turned slowly to look at her.

"Sorry," she said. "I didn't mean to startle you."

There was something in her voice, though, in the soft and looming expression that made me lower my guard. I had the strange sense of hearing my name whispered like a sigh in my ear. The face observing me was a simple one, distant, and the woman to whom it belonged was dragging a bag of trash, trying to camouflage, without too much fuss, the state of her shabby, soiled clothes.

It wasn't the first night I'd encountered her. I'd seen her on other occasions standing there, beside one of the high cement slabs that sustains our building, observing me, self-possessed. I'd seen some kids throw stones at her and laugh when she ran away. Obviously this was another thing that life in our housing unit didn't coax me into sharing.

"It's fine," I said. "I'm not afraid."

I liked to stay outside sometimes, to feel the block on its own, exclusive, to linger in the commons as if it were an enclave for me alone, that soft, tamed garden area that immobilized the block. And I liked to look for those colorful angels ("ignes fatuus," Valdemar corrected me), like the one I'd seen a few days before on my nightly walk; emerging, flutteringly, its scales aglow from amid the piles of jetsam like weeds in the common gardens. But I only ever told these things to Valdemar, never to strangers. Valdemar listened with his stick-in-the-mud logic, and everything returned to its rightful place, recovered its attributes.

That night, a specter of blue lights materialized amid the debris and I saw it disperse, stretch out, as if it were about to wink a mischievous eye at me from the high scrub grass.

"Do you believe in angels?" the woman said, dropping her bags next to mine.

I hesitated before answering, only because I want to respond the way Valdemar does with me. Finally I said:

"I suppose that before I can believe in them, I'd have to know exactly what they are."

My voice sounded like his, though not as deep, not as distant.

The woman nodded and I couldn't help smiling.

"You're a boy who's too grown up," she said, and her voice fractured suddenly, like a delicate Calliandra stem. "My little one, what have they done to you?"

Then instead of the calming effect, stirring me, her expression began to scare me. I took a few steps back; her afflicted stare tried to reach me in the emptiness spinning around us. We were both alone. A tingle in my hip was the only thing left of our nascent proximity. I tightened up like an archer's bow, and feeling compelled to meow, I howled with the sad voice of a boy who could wake up the entire unit, the entire block, all of New City. I gazed at her with the intensity of my yellow eyes. And this time, despite my fear, I didn't try to run away again.

Valdemar was seventy years old, and measured five feet four inches tall. Back in the day, his bone structure must have been solid, and he probably looked taller than he was. But old age, and even before that an illness in his hip, had caused him to walk with a straying sort of gait that made him self-conscious. Maybe that's why he lost interest in making friends with those in neighborhood and usually spent hours at a time at home, alone, going through the same hobbies and same old routines of which he'd never become bored. There he was, detained in time, until the day I came for a visit with my father, of course, and he started giving me arithmetic lessons. His wife, Serginha, had died eight years earlier, in a notorious accident that had happened in Free City; but I didn't find out about that for a while after he had died.

In the mornings, after Papá left for work, I'd go downstairs and knock at Madureira's door, punctually, to begin our lessons. Despite my fears, as the days went by I started having fun with him, and by the end of the first week I wasn't going only to study, but also to spend time chatting with him while Papá was away, always busy attending to things. Sometimes Madureira entertained me playing chess games he took from books: the game of twenty four movements that Baron Von Kempelen's automata used to beat Napoleon or some old card game strategies or physics tricks for building a propulsion boat or volcanoes and balloons that got away and drew long spirals outside our window. He gave me problems that I would solve out of pride, and when the first month came to an end, I continued visiting him to hear him talk about history or make me discover something new in one of the endless volumes that Serginha had left behind without dusting off.

And I went back home at night.

I read comic books in my bedroom, and then heated the leftovers Papá had cooked for the weekend suppers. I would set the table and wait for him to get home, overloaded with papers and stamps. We'd have dinner together, in silence, and say goodnight before going to sleep.

That's when I would hear the swishing sound of plastic being dragged against the cement, followed by sandals tapping the ground as if they were sluggishly applauding, slapping the wet ground that was carpeted in January drizzle before floundering their way down the stairs. Valdemar would laugh and try to scare me, saying they were souls from Purgatory that came to haunt the Earth. But they were only our neighbors, hauling their bags out to the wall of refuse. Papá usually came home from the neighborhood councils in a bad mood; he would turn on the television in the living room, and fall asleep in front of the blinking monitor. Some of the kids had gotten sick, it was true, and though the authorities announced negotiations and pending agreements, the union hadn't accepted any terms, and the garbage trucks were still snoozing beside the housing units in a standstill that had lasted nearly a month now.

"And while they're out getting drunk in Free City," I heard my father say, "what about us? The people who came to fill this flea-bitten city with honest work? What do these morons expect from us? That we throw ourselves to the rats?"

Papá echoed the same arguments I heard on the news— what the engineers said when they carped over deadlines and scheduling snafus—the neighbors acknowledged the complaints in the council meetings, argued against them and came to similar conclusions, and then they'd only go back to discussing something that had supposedly been resolved already and everything would start all over again. By the time Farinelli got to wailing even louder than before, I was able to save Papá's glasses from a particularly disturbing dream, and I went on listening to him, imagining Free City with something between fascination and fear.

The next day I brought it up with Valdemar. I asked him about Free City.

"Free City?" he replied with a question, surprised.

I told him about Papá's nightly complaining and how he'd repeat the same thing over and over again before falling asleep. I knew Valdemar had lived there years before, and wanted to know if it was as dangerous as they said.

"Anything is dangerous if other people say it is. The problem is whether it's true for the people who live there. The settlers flocked there with the mission of raising an entire city within two years. An entire city! Can you imagine what that means, little lamb? And the people who established themselves had to work from the esplanade of a dream that had only appeared in a prophecy, given by someone who lived far away from here. Nobody with that level of responsibility has time to do damage; though damage was done, of course. A tremor shakes all manner of stone. And though some went there to get rich at other people's expense, most of them didn't actually live in Free City. Things have changed since then. The city exists now. There are no new prophecies to pacify the population. No great cross, no Don Bosco's honey."

"And you worked in the city, right?" I insisted.

"Maybe," he said. "I built the city up, like everyone else. During the founding period, each one of us built up the part we were allotted as best we could. Then we inhabited the space, and continue fashioning it to our tastes. We had to tame the population, same as we had to tame the earth."

He stood up from the table and vanished for a few minutes into his bedroom. I heard him rummaging through his drawers, and he came back with a box in his hand.

"This is what I built," he said.

He opened the box: newspaper clippings; two medals fastened with faded ribbons; a few photos of him dressed in uniform beside wrinkled ghost-faces, some cropped at the edges. I recognized him standing tall halfway down a line of seven people, out of focus but recognizable; I pointed to him with my finger. "How old were you here?" I asked.

"Twenty-seven," he picked up a yellowed diploma that had a seal on it in the form of a watermark. "Second Officer," he read. "Valdemar Madureira. 43rd Squadron, Santa Genoveva. State of Minas Gerais."

"Same as Papá," I told him. "And my grandfather Gotardo. And my uncles and aunts, and my cousins, and the relatives I haven't seen since we left Juis de Fora one hurried morning that I can't even remember now."

"That's right," he answered. "Your father is a miner

like me, little lamb. Like you. Like so many of us who walk this earth. That's why we're not accustomed to being alone, though we are."

I looked at the belt he was wearing in the photograph and pointed to it.

"Where's your gun?"

Valdemar chuckled in a rolling way that seemed to clean his insides out.

"I sold it," he answered. "A long time ago."

But I suspected he was lying. A person doesn't easily divest of the things that define him. They're patent loyalties, even for the eight-year-old boy I was at that time. I couldn't have imagined getting rid of my puppets or my bicycle. I glanced toward the end of the room, the door was slightly ajar, and imagined the revolver, its well-worn alloy, though without scratches; its wooden handle, polished every morning with a circular, dogged patience. Enveloped in a green deerskin cloth, I imagined it hidden in a console in a bottom drawer, confused with other clothes and random accessories; other keepsakes he preferred not to mention; with his departed, stuffed in other boxes, open, buried. I shivered over these thoughts, and compassion, as if spilled from a glass, made me search his eyes. Surely Valdemar understood that I had shifted and transposed elements of his story. He sighed, as if all the nostalgia had suddenly exhausted him, and he brought the lesson to a close saying it was already very late. In truth it was only two. And the sky was blue and the sun radiated a mild light outside.

* * *

The next time Farinelli meowed his moaning charged the block with unusual intensity; he stretched his throat out as if it was boiling water, and the day before the lessons were over, I mentioned to Valdemar that something was amiss in our unit. Lately, Valdemar had been ending our lessons early. Once I finished solving problems on paper, he retired to his room; he said he was tired, and I could tell he was discouraged in some way. It wasn't the way he usually behaved, and though he opened his library to me, it wasn't the same when the books didn't pass first through his hands. That very afternoon, I delivered the monthly *cruzeiros* that Papá had entrusted to me. Seeing the results of my test, Professor Rovênia said that now I did my exercises quickly; and Papá could be proud of his son, and Valdemar had put the money away, in bills of twenty, in a little red bag whose hiding place he wasn't embarrassed to show me.

We didn't pick up on our previous conversation about Free City that afternoon. Valdemar preferred not to respond when I asked, and I respected his silence. He didn't pull out his old box of diplomas or sepia-tinted photographs full of ghosts this time, though I teased him every once in a while calling him "Sergeant," and he looked cheerful. Maybe it was this chumminess that allowed me to open up more. Whatever the reason, Valdemar asked me that afternoon, for the first time, about my mother. His eyes, wide and melancholy like big hurricane lamps seemed to peer out at me from a cracked photo, from someplace so far away that now it makes me shiver to think of it. I told him I couldn't recall what her face looked like (Papá had destroyed her photos when we settled here), and besides a checkered apron, or a hovering silhouette on a sunny afternoon where shining buckles of light scratched at her shadow, I had nothing else left of her. I explained that I had no memory of her, and these were the only images evoked when I thought about her. Even her name had stopped being familiar to me: Sara no longer signified Mamá. But I had recently begun to dream about her a lot, especially since seeing that woman in the commons and running away from her, when I scaled the stairs feeling her bittersweet breath on my neck.

But I was only eight years old then, Valdemar; and even though the words squeezed together in my bewilderment, they were actually too big for me to grab onto and wield; my explanation came as if it had spilled from a glass and I could see the heavy drops falling ever so slowly, but I was afraid to do anything about it, I lacked the courage to extend my hand into the air and tilt the glass upright.

"The point is that I can't see her," I said, but now I'm aware that I had said it like a boy who could see her but who hadn't yet learned how to choose his words correctly.

I told him what I was able to tell him at that age: that I no longer missed her, which according to Valdemar was a good thing. When you forget, my father told me, you leave little holes that you can fill with something new.

"Your father is a smart man." He stood up abruptly and went to fetch a bottle of spirits whose label was scratched off. "And he loves you very much, little lamb, more than you can imagine."

He had rubbed his eyes below his glasses; and they lit up as he filled his glass to look at me through a well-worn, murky reflection.

"Don't ever forget what I'm going to tell you right now." I saw him newly serious, and suddenly he was seventy years old again, doing a shot, the fire of it clearing out his throat: "I'm old enough by now to leave an inheritance; but I've never had anyone to give it to. So I'm going to give it to you. Sometimes you have to cut something for beautiful things to grow. Sometimes sacrifice is the only way to find beauty, happiness, and order. There's a hidden balance behind everything we do, and at times those who love you are able to see it, and they're the ones who have the responsibility of choosing for you when you haven't yet figured it out on your own."

He poured himself another shot and swished it around to let it breathe a little, for the smell of the warm alcohol to calm the beast.

"For example, the Great Man knew that when he sent us to this gritty, hostile place to forge a new country from scratch. He *had* to do it. If he didn't take the initiative, nobody else would have, and his leap of faith moved others to follow suit, the ones who with their bare hands, built the ground you're standing on now. And here we are, yessiree, so many years later; living, enjoying, and despising one other. It's a difficult choice for a parent to make, don't you think? Fathers and sons end up hating each other because they don't understand each other. And what they don't understand is that this is the order of things that will sustain what others have resigned themselves to building; being guided by other people's faith, even if it means having something taken from us that we love."

He scratched the tip of a beard that sprung from his face like an ambush, making his words seem older and not so much his age.

He remained lost in thought.

"It's been a while since I've dreamed," he says. "Every morning since Serginha died, I wake up feeling empty. I wish I could see her sometimes, like you your mother. But if she doesn't appear, it must be because she doesn't want to see me again."

I told him that I could dream about him, and if it worked, it would mean that he was dreaming too.

Valdemar laughed sadly, accepting the false logic hidden in my words. "I know you'll do it, little lamb." And then, ponderingly, "It's probably not such a bad thing not to dream anymore. It's as if every morning I were given the chance to start over again."

Yes, I respond. We could start over, Valdemar. And

I kept saying it as I walked up the stairs; and I continued saying it after eating in silence with Papá, when I ended up in bed trying to dream about my friend. Tonight I would dream about the woman who dragged her giant black bags to set them next to mine. I would dream about my proud father and the huge family waiting for me impatiently in Juiz de Fora. And in all these dreams, Farinelli would stretch his meows, weaving the air full of angels, in turquoise and blue, and Mamá would hold out her hand, and she wouldn't cry over me, or my father, or the boy who had become a man.

But Farinelli didn't wail that night. And it was the silence, not the sound of my father's steps, that woke me from the darkness. The cement slabs seemed to buckle under a mineral groan, as if the whole block were rousing from some raucous, disturbing dream. I got up and looked out the window to see huge, slow-moving metal bodies. I moved, too, without realizing it, from below several layers of clothing, and saw myself scuttling down the stairs and out to the ground level behind them. Some of the neighbors were chattering along the edges, tying to make themselves heard over the noise of the motors. The dozers of the lower ranks of the police were opening a path on the other side of our barricade of black bags, and the lights shone in like a liberating force that no one was happy to see. Other lights twirled like *ignes fatuus*, but the ones that drew our attention were fake *ignes fatuus*:

the ones whose sirens were off, the ones that stroked our red and blue faces behind a newly demarcated barrier of yellow tape.

"A dead woman," I heard an old woman walking towards us say between sobs, before an officer shooed her away, his arms extended in the shining light, dispersing curious onlookers like a big cross in the middle of the road.

Guided by the voices of others, I could make out the contours of a black bag the police were guarding as they waited for the coroner to show up, and a hand on one of the sides of the bag that had just yielded to its pressure, dangled like a black and blue swath of cloth floating in the air.

But I didn't look at her like everyone.

I preferred to look up.

Bossa Nova for Chico Pires Duarte

Oh, if I were to tell you about life,
there'd be blood on its hands;
not the red smears—of painted lips
or party kisses.

Oh, if I were to tell you about life,
there›d be its simple death,
not a bright flame—looming hot
over one who sleeps awaiting.

Bossa nova, v. 1, 2.
COLLECTION OF POPULAR SONGS IN THE FAVELAS OF RIO DE
JANEIRO, MARCELA FONSECA COSTA, 1991

CHICO PIRES DUARTE slowed his pace at the first corner,
on Rúa Conde de Bonfim, and looked back down the
long, vacant street barely lit by the streetlights. A colloi-
dal liquid akin to fog seemed to spill over the houses and
hold them afloat in the rain, like a band of shipwrecked

sailors clutching at pieces of debris to keep from sinking. Calmly now (he knew they were no longer behind him, that he'd given them the slip), Pires Duarte avoided the road to Flamengo, sticking to the plan he'd devised long before murdering Pinheiro, and cut straight across the shanty town at the foot of São Clemente Hill, to hide out in a shack in the South Zone. Yellow lights drowned out a sense of time there, too: floating dense and gummy like on the steep slope.

He imagined Old Eduardo again without much trouble, who had accompanied him all the way down, seated beside him, listening to his tale: his awkward hand looking for a place in the kitchen; the leaky, corrugated iron roof wobbling against the storm whose cavernous moaning sucked everything outwards. He saw his sleeve, blood stained and rolled to the elbow, and he saw Pinheiro's face, too, at the crack of dawn, at that instant when, still dazed and ashen, he finally made sense of all the barking he'd heard throughout the night. How long had they been there? One, maybe two hours? How long since Chico had fallen silent, leaving him alone with his own thoughts? Pires Duarte's eyes adjusted to his surroundings, behind a tangle of smoke unraveling in front of his face. He suspected there was a sleepless night, or deep sleep, or that young body's infinite exhaustion, in that angle of the unlit room. In rhythmic agony, Old Eduardo's cigarette finally burned to the end, between his fingertips. He heard the creak of a door and tracked it impatiently to somewhere outside the shack. It was dawn.

Eduardo eyed the smoke slipping listlessly from the last carroty flare, and listened to the murmur of voices in the background pick up again, as if on tiptoe. He observed the brilliant disc from the darkness: the dawn sky opening its yawning mouth over a horizon split in two, stretching out along the line of earth as if someone had just gouged a colossal chunk from it and left it to bleed out, an open, crimson wound behind Rio's flora.

The door he'd hardly been able to see last night was behind him now, bruised by the humidity; the tiny, bowed figure of a woman and the refuge, the entire night reduced to simple wooden partitions, buckets and tires, dirt floors. The woman ambled behind him; Eduardo imagined her for a second: toothless, dark hands dripping down the door without looking him in the eye. "Nobody wants to mess with Pinheiro's guys," he thought. Not hard to imagine. Outside, the weather floated in the new dawn like a dense layer of fog. It reeked of mothballs, old rags, and the slow decay that reduces everything to dust. Still squinting before the shining sky that was just beginning to break into clouds, Chico Pires Duarto gazed at the closed doors and slowly the terror of being alone crept in. Suddenly gripped by the realization, he thought: "Marcinho must be out beating the bushes by now. They're scouring São Clemente Hill for me."

"He came here afterwards," the old man said.

Chico Pires Duarte breathed out a long current of smoke and for the first time his gaze focused in the penumbra. He noticed the light sneaking out from the interiors like a complicit wink above the door. He sensed movement, a few shadows slipping here and there; but time wasn't on his mind any longer: he heard voices and chairs being dragged heavily against the floor's wooden planks. By now, Old Eduardo had fallen silent before the strength of his tale, his voice had dissolved into the haze redolent of tobacco and wet wood floating about his face.

"I arrived at dusk," Pires Duarte nodded. "I came looking for Fernanda Abreu."

Old Eduardo's hands sketched a gesture in disagreement.

"You're too young and reckless to understand things yet, but let me tell you something. Life is worth a lot more than you think. Murdering Pinheiro was foolhardy, the worst thing you could have done," he added, and his eyes shone with a watery flare. "You really think a woman is worth dying for?"

"Fernanda isn't a woman," he snapped, as if it'd been on his mind a long time before replying. "She's just a dream."

The old man coughed out a gruff laugh and a gob of spit.

"I'm serious, boy."

Chico Pires replied calmly, "You've lived longer than me, Eduardo. Seen a lot more of life. There will always be people who kill for country, for honor, or for who knows what other useless dream. Even for God. To die for a woman, Eduardo . . . What difference does it make the name you give the dream? Doesn't make it more real or fleeting."

Old Eduardo knew him enough to realize that this time he wasn't pretending. Chico Pires Duarte had been hanging around ever since that afternoon a long time ago, when Eduardo was playing the viola over in the middle barrio, on Oswaldo Seabra, and that baby face of his just froze on the spot, listening spellbound to the sounds he was scratching out on the strings. How could he tell him now that his music was nothing but a beautiful lie? How to explain the responsibility he felt over his fortune in life? His rough, leathery hands came together in the penumbra, bending like branches in the wind. How could he tell him now that the stories of heroes and lovers he'd sung to him were nothing more than beautiful lies, nothing but music and lyrics so they would never exist?

"Oh, Chico Pires Duarte," he thought. "If I were to tell you truly about life . . ." The sun, like a ball of fire then, appeared again between his fingers; it flared for a moment, then tempered, and before long a cloud of smoke wafted in between. Peals of laughter announced a cotton-mouthed, boozy presence somewhere; maybe in the next room.

They heard footsteps, the scrape of a door, and the suddenly voices fell silent.

Pires Duarte felt something brush his shoulder.

"There's still time to get away from here, Chico."

He heard the old man's difficult breathing rasp the damp air.

"You could reconcile with the family if that's what you want . . . maybe if you give it some time, a few months . . . There are always so many angles, and people who will benefit by his death. But not right now, see? There's too much honor at stake for you to stay here tonight, too many facades and appearances to be kept up . . ."

He knew it was useless to insist, that the boy Pires was never going to leave; but he had to try.

Shortly, though, the old man settled back down in his chair and looked up. "I get why you won't leave, I think," he said.

In truth, he'd understood it all the second he'd opened the door and found him sitting on that bench, where he still was now.

"You're waiting for them to kill you too, aren't you, Pires Duarte? That's why you're here tonight, in this room, talking to me."

It didn't long for him to answer this time, either.

"Yeah," he said, lazily. "That's why I'm at Pinheiro's deathwatch."

2.

Fernanda watched Chico's image multiply in the vanity mirror, and was hit with a revelation she'd already begun to intuit after the first orgasm months earlier, only now it came like a flash out of the blue, irreconcilably, a feeling akin to someone telling her they'd found a malignant tumor in her body and confessing that there was nothing to be done. Chico Pires Duarte was a strong, good-looking mulatto, with features almost too fine even for a white man's face. But now everything that had been invented with him seemed that afternoon to have been a deliberate mistake, not only the features of his fine face—clearly the mere invention of this beautiful creature who stood in front of her right now, pulling on his corduroy trousers, accommodating his hard body into the folds at his inner thighs, was a sort of wild dream meant to provoke a calamitous situation. She watched him button his trousers, then settle on the edge of the bed to tie his sneakers so neatly. She watched his ritual affectionately this time, no longer feeling the exasperation of a few hours earlier during foreplay, when Chico started undressing with the same calm meticulousness.

"You always handle things so delicately . . ." she said, thinking out loud, "so slowly and gently, that sometimes I think it's the only reason I like being with you. To feel, if only for a few hours, that nothing bad can happen to me; by your side, no danger could exist."

Chico›s lips traced a condescending smile from the other side of the mirror, and he twisted around and kissed her on the lips. Fernanda didn't resist, she let herself be kissed, though she really didn't feel like it. She was trying to fashion a response, and her reflection was merely a means to formulating a question, not a concession, not a gesture of love, not a sudden show of weakness. So she lay back on the pillow while Chico finished buttoning his shirt and threw his hair into a makeshift ponytail, and finally stood before the wrinkled sheets from where her two breasts peeked out like a pair of curious creatures.

"So," she went on after a pause, "I just don't get why you won't seriously consider Guilherme's offer in São Paulo. How come someone sensitive like you doesn't want to get out of the favela? Why not ditch this place and find a decent life somewhere else; someone who does things so gently, why won't you spend a few seconds considering it, the way you do when you button your trousers and tie your shoes, think of the advantages a factory job can offer you . . . Chico, are you listening to me? Will you please explain yourself?"

3.
"Chico?" Pinheiro asked. "The fuck you doing here?"

4.
Chico Pires Duarte dug his hand into the pocket of his pants in case someone showed up on Rúa Carvalho. He stood and fondled the knife, though his fingers didn't react with the same reassurance when they scratched its shape, the leather handle, the silvery blade he imagined infinitely beautiful ensconced in the corduroy. It wasn't an innate sense of self-confidence or even the fear that visited him on certain lonely nights on the Hill that made

him stop at that particular bend in road, that wouldn't let him leave without first killing Pinheiro. Smoking had never been a habit, yet tonight he'd bought a pack of blonde tobacco in case it got cold while he waited. He had only ever smoked a little. The smoke he exhaled might warn them that he was there, in wait, at the bend on Rúa Carvalho. Since he didn't smoke enough, it might make him cough, there are people who think you can tell, intuit, even suspect death, especially when it's not the result of age, but of circumstance. "To kill a man is to carry out an act of optimism," he thought, "an errand that is too great. A feat that only brings fear when you don't think that at the same time, there's room for victory over guilt."

5.

"What did you say? They killed Pinheiro?"

"Yes, Sir," the boy answered. "They slit him five times; killed him only once, on the fourth, in the right lung."

6.

Old Eduardo wondered whether the others weren't still behind him, or if they'd lost him, as what seemed like dust from the slope's balmy air fluttered about his ears. But this was a long time later, when Chico Pires confirmed that Fernanda hadn't arrived. So still had time; nobody knew that Pinheiro was dead yet. He ran out the minutes that were left, concentrating his attention on the broken line in the road that swayed quickly. Pires Duarte's eyes were fixed to the ground, watching his feet disappear and reappear again with each step hitting the pavement.

As he made his way in the rain, he saw that the lights to the shack on Oswald Seabra weren't on, as they had arranged the night before. Fernanda must be there, asleep; she'd jump up quickly, he'd hug her tightly; she'd have waited anxiously for him to show up. How could he not find her there, if São Paulo, if our life together? If Pinheiro was dead . . . He moved along the outer wall anxiously. He glanced around, crossed the street; the blonde light of the streetlamps dangled like spider's webs, like spilled honey. He glided at a different pace, a different time, dense and glutinous, and still in the adrenalin of his earlier charge, he now walked cautiously towards the door. *How long had he waited?*

The echoes of a dog barking followed him uphill as Chico approached the door and knocked. His heart beat hard in his chest as he tapped the door, over and over again, each time a little harder; but Fernanda Abreu never showed up, the old man ventured. She'd changed her mind, she'd abandoned him. The sun then, a puff of smoke, a gesture of acquiescence with his hands. Maybe she needed more time, Eduardo. He lay down on the ground, winded, panting. Maybe she didn't get away in time.

7.

"Don't be such a fool," Fernanda shouted. "You're the only thing I care about in this world . . . the only thing that matters; but you know perfectly well that given the chance to get out of here, I wouldn't hesitate. I'd pack my bag and be on that bus and wouldn't even think of you; I'd bite my lips, I'd keep my eyes closed till the end of the line; I wouldn't look back till I knew I was far away from this place."

"You could come with me."

"You know I can't," she replied.

"Well maybe you *could*," Chico said. "And not just *could*, maybe you *should*. You should leave your husband and come away with me to São Paulo. Tomorrow, on the first bus . . ."

"I can't," she interrupted. "You know that I can't do it."

8.

"You can't do it like that," one of the three of them mumbled, in case Pires Duarte came to, regained consciousness from the cloud of dust. "You just can't. Once they're down, you shoot for the head. Like this. Paf! Aim for the head. Get it?"

"Sure."

"We're good then," the other one said. "Now wake him up; fuckin cold out here."

"Yeah," Marcinho muttered, thinking, "How many folks gonna hear the shots tonight? Three shots. Nobody's gone recognize you, asshole." Three shots. Bang, bang, bang.

"Come on, I don't got all the time in the world, man."

They wake him up.

"Chico . . ." Marcinho says, pulling his arm, "Chico . . ."

9.

"Hey Sugar!" Pinheiro shouted. "Come here now, woman, don't be shy. That's right . . . over here . . . come on. See this fine gentleman here? Why don't you give him a kiss, dear. Yeah, a welcome kiss. Don't be shy now boy . . . you neither, yeah, that's it . . ."

"*Encantado*," Chico said, falling into his seat.

"Francisco Pires. And this is my wife, Fernanda."

"Jesus!" she smiled, flustered. "So now we get all serious, huh? What's all this about? I'm supposed to greet all your friends by kissing them now?"

"Just this once . . ." Pinheiro said. "Just this once, Sugar. This gentleman here is in love with *la señora*."

Pinheiro took a long pull of his drink and held his tongue. His silence was as bitter as the sound of his voice after a shot of grain alcohol. He calculated the time it would take for his words to nick at Pires's will. He laughed silently, pleased at how his bravado had confused him. Laughed self-satisfied at his own imagination, his cold blood.

"No harm in giving a little gift of wishful thinking every once in a while, Sugar."

The fingers of one hand smoothed the side of his moustache; with the other he grabbed the woman around her waist, sat her on his knees and kissed her on the lips.

"See boy, as long as it's not a sexual thing, I don't mind her being your goddess," he said. Now suddenly serious, he started twirling his class of *cachaca* with little flicks of his wrist. "I don't care if she's your goddess, long as it's in your head, something in your dreams; because she's your goddess, and that's what she's meant to be for you or for Marcinho or any other piece of shit in this place, you understand?"

"Señor Pinheiro," Chico stuttered, quick to answer, "I didn't mean any offense . . ."

Pinheiro told him to shut up with a gesture of his hand.

He looked at Fernanda again, who was standing still beside the door, looking amused.

"See that?" Pinheiro smiled, patting his stomach confidently. "Tonight you're a goddess, Sugar. Go ahead now, check up on the kids."

She was wearing a blue and white polka-dot dress with little folds in the sleeves that bared her thin, strong arms.

"Just don't keep your goddess waiting too long tonight," she said on her way out.

They heard giggles in the hallway, footsteps, and a little later the sound of the door snapping shut.

Chico was getting ready to answer, when the other stopped him in his tracks.

"Don't be stupid, boy," Pinheiro's voice rasped, with authority, over the sound of the music. "Everyone's got a working rod around here, got it? Sooner or later though, it just stops working. It's an age thing."

Pinheiro fell quiet, mulling over what he'd just said. Sure, life's tough. One day you're king of the hill, and the next, some mistake, some betrayal, takes you down, way below where you were before. *A man's life is like the story of his own dick. Strong men get hard over and over again till they don't.*

"Yessir," Pinheiro breathed. "A man's life is nothing but constant struggle."

He pushed the remote control and the volume of the music rose until it drowned out the sounds from the street.

"As for you, boy," he said after a while, changing his tone, "you can do whatever you want with your life. With your head, too. But you listen up close, don't you try to pull anything stupid in front of my eyes. Tonight I let you kiss Fernanda, consider it a gift, so you can measure how far away from her you are. Because I'll cut your balls off and make you swallow them, I ever catch you or hear about you looking at her the way you did tonight when you walked into my home . . ."

"Señor," Chico responded, "didn't mean no offense . . ."

"Now knock off the stupidity," Pinheiro said, and pulled a tiny scale out of his desk drawer.

10.

"And that's how he ended up here," the old man nodded, moving his gnarled hands, like those of a tired animal, knowingly across the frets, the deaf rumor losing itself in the instrument's hollow.

A ghostly suicide, tumbling down the wooden slope, he thought, *falling, falling,* falling until it vanished altogether, a static silence dismissed his voice, and the sounds of the guitar faded like an echo surrendered in the depths of his open eyes. The stark heat waned as dusk fell, looming over the cracked asphalt, and his hat rested beside his legs like an upside-down turtle shell, a few coins reflecting the last rays of the sun from the bottom of the fabric. His trousers were soiled, and his sandals exposed his panting feet and their worn nails that had lost their form and color over time. The skin of his face, deeply toasted by the suffocating summer past, held out like a scar under the shadow of his thinning hair. How time flies, he thought. And scratched out a chord on the guitar that resounded in his hands like something alive, but ailing. He'd made a concession this time, when the people listening to him play asked about Pires Duarte. All he'd usually do now is recap the story, the one he'd made up for him seven years ago when he sang the bossa nova so as not to let him die altogether, that's what he did each time someone asked, like now, for him to tell the true story of his death.

Playing the same chord as always, making his fingers skip deftly over the strings, he sang:

Oh, if I were to tell you about life,
you'd have blood on your hands:
no stains so red—as painted lips,
or party kisses

As he strummed and his gritty voice spilled down the walls and the deep cliff, as if he had seen him just yesterday, as near as the short night he accompanied him to Pinheiro's house, old Eduardo looked again at the shadows gathering around door, nearing the end, and his tale, this time without Chico Pires Duarte's voice, was about nor more than the struggle that never came, and to the whisper in the ear that did come, and was completed the afternoon following his death.

Did he make a run for it?

"No," the old man answered. And waited bravely in his chair until he felt someone closing in, and heard a warm, gravelly voice murmur something in his ear; it was the voice he had been waiting for, really, since he arrived at the shack to know why he'd been called to Pinheiro's deathwatch. As they guided him towards the yellow light that sketched the exterior bricks in the middle sector, near the slope of Rúa Conde de Bonfim, Chico Pires Duarte closed his eyes and imagined that one of the passing glints of gray, one of the shadows in the street, was her. Maybe he would have liked for Fernanda to come out to him, it's something the old man would never be able to know, and anyway, it was much better to think he hadn't wished for that.

Damn, he thought, walking out towards the street. He'd never felt better in his life. This time he was immense and solid, more than other nights, as he allowed himself to be pulled slowly towards the street. A final push and before vomiting next to that yellow light floating around the streetlights, he looked behind, at the people walking out of the shack, and then he looked at Marcinho holding in his hands the gun that days earlier he had also maneuvered, alert, with that sure aim that had been so satisfying to him Pinheiro. He looked at him caringly, or feeling pity, or feeling endless fear. Because, like him, so many times in Pinheiro's care, tonight Marchinho's acts were justified.

Chico Pires Duarte thought, without hesitating, following the others down the street, "Just aim for the head."

Oz

This last nerve of yours, so fine
is made soul
El otro Asterión, José Watanabe

For Micaela Chirif

THE TIN MAN CRACKED his old joints so I could hear
them. The sound was like a walnut being splintered in
a nutcracker, or between a strong set of molars. He used
to do it constantly. Crack nuts that is, not just walnuts,
and he'd always offer me the best part of the meat. But
eventually he stopped doing it. He simply quit, and I
resigned myself to the fact that walnuts and other dried
fruits would no longer be part of my diet. Now, T.M. and
I listen to his querulous metal joints, buckling like some
old hand-me-down thing that doesn't even close properly. And just when I think it's over, I hear him pop the
rickety old hinges in an even shriller pitch, as if this time,
surely, he means to collapse altogether.

"What's going on?" I ask.

I find him toiling at the end of the dining room, bending an arm upwards and then downwards, as if he were trying to extract water from some invisible well. After thirty minutes of forcing me to listen to him grind away like that, the only thing he's accomplished is for me to set aside my newspaper impatiently, and for his voice to begin spilling out with a hollow resonance that at another time even I might have described as sullen.

"I think there's something wrong with me," T.M. says.

Seeing him manipulate that makeshift artificial skeleton strikes me as pitiful but I don't tell him that.

"Nothing unusual," I say reassuringly. "It had to happen sooner or later."

"What, Harumi?"

"Growing old."

The Tin Man shakes his head.

"I think I'm getting rusty."

As if fact were proof of his hypothesis, he wriggles the bolts in his forearms again and hears their sharp objection, once, twice, three times, before stopping. No more doubt. He repeats the gesture with the rest of his body, and a moment later we have to admit that things don't appear to be any better than they did before.

"Will death be like this?"

"I don't know," I say to him.

"What do you mean you don't know?" he scolds. "You're supposed to know everything."

We had this conversation a long time ago, if my memory serves. But I'm old now, and exhausted, and I realize he'll never believe what I tell him, no matter how many times I say it. Soon, I won't even believe it myself: I'll have forgotten everything I've ever told him. And that's the truth of this story.

"I don't know," I say again, shamefully, and go back to my newspaper.

"Well you should."

T.M. continues cracking his old tin backbones as if he hasn't heard a thing I said, just to aggravate me.

There once was a time when T.M. and I were the center of attention. We traveled to Emerald City, and a reputation for being invincible. The Tin Man played chess and I barked challenges to others who could play, unfolding a chair in the middle of the square, any square, where I arranged the pieces on a small chessboard table, and waited for someone, anyone, to place their bets into the sizeable top hat that had once belonged to my great grandfather. We were never at a loss for troublemakers and rabble-rousers. I mean, what else can be expected in a city. Gentlemen left chess playing a long time ago in favor of more lucrative trades, so out on the street it wasn't their persuasion that we encountered. There's a vague human conceit that makes it impossible to accept defeat at the hands of the gadget, whatever the make or model. To lose to an object is like losing to one's own self; carefully considered, it's the toughest form of defeat for a human to digest. It didn't take long before T.M. was used to winning, and the machine's celebrity spread like a tide across the county. He played with me at first, practicing and improving his game; but soon he outdid even my skills, which weren't nothing, and we decided it was time to venture outside of the city limits, make our fortune and come back, sooner rather than later, to settle down. I wasn't entirely mistaken. The hat filled with luminous victories, and our itinerary eventually spread to eight more counties, stealing forth like a man's reputation when it's charged with something more than the shadow left he behind in his own land.

One evening a man who went by the name Euwe showed up in Emerald. I extended my hand in greeting and the damp chafe of his handshake warned me that he would be trouble. Euwe's thick red moustache sprung like something electric from his face, and the spectacle of his politeness wore one's nerves thin within minutes.

"They tell me your mechanical monkey is invincible," he said.

He came with a peculiar, entourage: a woman with bawdy makeup clutching his elbow, and two mammoth black men in green suits and coarse manners.

"That's right," I answered, paying no mind to the swagger. "As far as I know, no regular monkey has ever been able to beat him."

Euwe smirked.

"That's why I'm here, my dear gentleman."

He slipped his coat off and left it floating over the chair. Aside from a fat woman sweeping the hallway floors, he and his coterie were the only callers at the inn.

"I challenge you."

His goading couldn't have come at a more inopportune time. I had an appointment with Dr. Gustav Grumblat in less than an hour. Long before winter arrived, Dr. Grumblat had already reserved a time to pit himself against T.M., hoping that by then some defect in my machine's game might have shown up, some fault in its subterfuge. The chance for another go had cost the doctor a wad of bills, substantially more than the first time around, and I explained as much to Euwe. It was hard to renege on so sweet a deal as Grumblat's, and it was my only chance to convince him that the Tin Man wasn't just another Old World quack transported to this part of the Earth. I told him we'd be back by eleven, at which time both the mechanical monkey and I would be delighted to attend to his bid; but something in Euwe's eyes flashed a blunt, cautionary murkiness and I saw him slip his hand into his pocket.

I was sure he was drawing a gun, but instead he flashed a fat wad of bills and spread them like a deck of cards.

"Somehow you're not catching my drift," Euwe said, placing his money on top of the table. "I've journeyed some four hundred miles in order to show this here lady how a man's genuine artfulness doesn't lie in imitating intelligence, but in putting it into practice."

My attention suddenly focused on the woman, on the layer of goo plastered across her face for whiter skin, and it dawned on me that it was her and not her chaperone or his henchmen that I should be worried about.

I relented.

I glanced at my pocket watch and imagined optimistically that in thirty minutes T.M. will have cracked Euwe's bravado. With a little luck, Dr. Grumblat would accept an apology. With a little savvy, we might even profit by this scene that was already turning out to be annoying. What a great excuse to leave the city, I thought, a notion I hadn't considered until then and yet suddenly, that night, it seemed a perfectly logical plan.

I salaamed and ran up to my room to look for T.M.

I found him in the living room, staring at a bee that wove pentagonal shapes while unsuccessfully trying to cross through the window's glass.

"I need thirty additional minutes," I said, awaiting him in the doorway. "Thirty more, or however much you need, before the game with Grumblat. Then it's back home. I promise."

If anyone asked me how I started betting with T.M., I wouldn't know what to say. I believe it was out of necessity; but the real reason is lost in the deteriorating synapses of my brain, which have taken the early years of my youth away, and with them the whole T.M. project before he became the accident he is now. Maybe I could use a story, someone else's story to plug into the absence of my own. I have the suspicion, though, that I've already done that once.

Two days ago I came across a book in my library and read it with delight, surprised to be inadvertently repeating an old pleasure. The margins were brimming with notes jotted in my own handwriting, though all of it seemed so strange to me. The story was simple, anyway. There was a chess playing automata dressed like a Turk, a famous watchmaker from the Viennese court, and one Johann Nepomuk Maelzel. The machine traveled the world for half a century performing its peculiar gift. It had been on a winning streak until the day they caught it in a small town near Baltimore. Someone began screaming for help, so that by the time the people causing the racket knew what had happened, it was already too late: a crowd had gathered. The cries issued from a familiar-looking wooden box. Without a carpenter on hand, a cabinetmaker was called, and from the belly of the relic, whose fanciful walls were mirror-lined, they pulled out a dwarf that was half-dead from asphyxiation. I imagine you know the tale.

That day Johann Nepomuk Maelzel swapped being celebrated as the last heir of Baron Von Kempelen's artifact, for being branded a swindler. Few people, not even the piercing Poe, had been able to admire the marvelous mechanism; its secret was lost forever the day it succumbed to a fire and was reduced to ashes in a Philadelphia museum. Nobody has ever been able to hide from one man the marvelous nature of another as astutely as him, while at the same time exposing to him his own wretchedness.

That's what I conveyed to Euwe that night, as he filled his fists with the money from the top hat: three months of itinerant bets gone in five minutes. I also let him know that he had the privilege of being the first person to witness an anomaly of perfection. Didn't that calamity remind him of an old and vanished myth? Wasn't there something familiar about that primitive life emerging from an error, negligible, invisible, and willing to forever contaminate the perfection of a stationary paradise?

Of course, Euwe paid me no mind.

When I was finally squared up, he grabbed his hat and coat and I never saw him again. But the two black men spent nearly an hour walloping on me while their owner smoked one after another of her long, delicate cigarettes. I still recall how that woman found a certain amount of pleasure in the spectacle; squinting her eyes as she inhaled; not quite smiling exactly, but as if she were. Those men kicked me hard till their own bodies were sore. At least I want to believe as much, though I'm pretty sure they were just waiting for the lady to finish her cigarettes. I have no idea how many she lit: she'd smoke one down to the filter and then light another. At the end of the night, or the break of the new day (here my memory gets hazy), her high-heeled shoe finally crushed the last butt into the ground, and I was left with five broken ribs and a jaw shattered into thirteen little pieces. They dragged me back to the inn like a piece of my own debris, and abandoned me there to ring up a new debt for the three months and two weeks it took before I was able to head home.

"You remember that afternoon when Euwe beat you in Emerald?" I ask the Tin Man.

The sound of his joints ceases momentarily. For the first time in a long while, I hear the friction of two little legs playing at being a violin—a cricket, perhaps, lost in the garden—and through them I see T.M.'s eyes moving through the feeble barrier that separates us, like a lantern.

"Yes," he says, without moving. "That was a long time ago."

"I guess they thought I was a swindler," I say.

"Maybe that's what you really were."

"That doesn't matter," I answer, uneasily. "We all end up cheating ourselves, one way or another."

"How do you mean?"

"For example, that night"—I fold the newspaper and set it on the side of the shelf—"I was sure you would win. Or at least that you would beat Grumblat. And we would leave the city with a small fortune in our hat."

Later I learned that the woman's name was Carol.

Carol Grumblat. And that she had spent a fortune for Euwe to travel from the north and beat the living daylights out of me, a job which her two men finished with such professional flare.

"There's just one thing I've never understood," I say, as if fishing for T.M. to answer me. "Why didn't she want you to play against her father? That's what I would like to know. At least before I forget the whole story anyway." I look over at the sill, at the window open to the night sky, and close my eyes as if I could find the answer out there, far away. "Why did I ever accept Euwe's challenge in the first place?"

T.M. remained silent, and when I open my eyes, I see him playing with his two hands. He discovered that his fingers can braid together and that they'll crack if he moves them.

"Why did you let him win?" I interrupted him.

There's no doubt in my mind about that. Never was, and I've come up with several hypotheses over these fifteen years that now T.M. should be able clarify, at least now that he's stopped cracking nuts.

"I don't know," he says.

"Were you upset that I didn't give you the night off, like I had promised?"

The cricket left us alone for a second, but I hesitate before realizing it and when I do, his little legs start rubbing together again; they've begun their own soundless sound.

"I guess I didn't want to die," T.M. says. "But thinking about it now, I'm not so sure anymore."

There's one thing I'm sure of: I like the new T.M. because he lets me win at chess. I know he does, because losing makes him feel strangely happy, the same way that winning makes me feel strangely alive. I reckon each of these flaws signifies one and the same thing, but I wouldn't venture to share this thought with him, at least not out loud, because lately T.M. has been very sensitive to definitions, to exactitudes, like a little boy discovering his surroundings; as if their strict denotation, and his inability to fit them into the logic of the world itself, hadn't already been undermined by having to meekly defer their expression to the few words we possess.

I didn't examine him that day when he refused to crack a walnut. Why should I have? That afternoon he had drawn a few pictures that others would have considered interesting. It's not his soul that worries me. I knew he was learning, that's all. I was never able to give him a heart and now that he had one, I wasn't able to take it away. Nothing else really matters. I had ceremonies in mind, not necessities. I'm an old man, and I have no children or friends who aren't already dead. All I ever needed was company. But I'm only aware of it now that I'm beginning to forget even my own name. In some sense, T.M.'s going broke signaled the start of my life's great new project. I mean, it had been a long time since I read the newspaper; all I listened to was his voice.

My hands discovered their suppleness and my eyes adjusted a little better to the daylight. I made the effort to walk. And that same afternoon I walked without crutches until my legs got tired. Now I walk to the kitchen and listen with renewed fascination to the sound of coffee pouring into my cup, making its way through the heat of its grains, like a tepid morning shower trickling over my shoulders. These are the times when I feel little more for him than a deep sense of gratitude for becoming human. For becoming what I am slowly but surely forgetting to be myself.

"There's a syndrome," I say, begging his attention for the first time that evening.

T.M. leans on the couch and looks at me with curiosity.

"Cotard delusion," I say, and add, "I think you're fascinated with the idea of being dead."

I had just woken up beside the newspaper, and saw the Tin Man as if he were a murky mirage, a torrent washing through the street after a stormy night. It took me a second to recognize him: Alzheimer's, the doctor told me, is like a filter that unravels one's perception of the world; like a candle that melts its own wax, as if the sufferer had to pay a price for having lived too long. I watched him through that rheumy membrane, my worn-out brain turning to sap, but I recognized him. He kept popping his arm as if he were ready to throw it out of joint, stubborn in that cracker-snapping sound that reverberated throughout the entire room.

"You won't die easily," I say, aware of the drowsiness edging up my spine. The dwarf who lives inside of you and moves your pieces would have to die first.

The Tin Man gets it: he's no fool.

As I experience decline, I find it peculiar how the brain selects the first images that will survive the stages of deterioration. I can't remember my mother's name, and yet I have an image from a dream, something that happened fleetingly during my recovery time at the inn. I'm sitting in front of T.M. and another machine like him moves a pawn, two squares towards the center of the board, to face the king. I know that I built them both, and now I'm waiting for them to finish the game they began at my behest. I don't know how long I'll be there. All I know is that neither one of them is able to lose.

I ask help to get up, and T.M. obliges, on the condition that I go into greater detail.

I agree, more out of need than good will on my part. The only thing I know for sure is that my back is aching and I wish to lie down in my bedroom. Something there makes me comfortable: something sensory, automatic; a smell, a reflection, maybe an angle. As he helps me walk, I try to recall the first lights that turned the Tin Man on, maybe right here. But the image doesn't come.

"Is this what death will be like?"

I'm in bed and hear its wooden structure creak as it accommodates my body.

Oh I can imagine death, yes I can. And for a minute I pretend that I actually remember it, and the inkling of it spatters my face like a raindrop. What will happen when I no longer expect it anymore, when my whole life, in that instant that gives volume to the past, empties out to become linear, transparent, perhaps like it is right now for T.M.? There's no answer to such a simple, logarithmic equation that could imbue a creature made of cables and fluids with life, like a negation of itself. You exist because you could not exist. That's not enough? I wonder if it hasn't always been this way: it's a lot easier to live because we die, or to remember because we forget, or to speak simply because we know that someone, at some point, will order us to shut up.

"I don't know," I say again.

"I'm curious to know," T.M. says, "that's all."

"In your case, it's simple," I say, stroking the hard texture of his apparatus, already timeworn and battered for the lack of maintenance he's had to endure since I began forgetting things.

I feel ashamed to hear his neck creak when he nods, but say not a word.

Instead, I point to a small heart-shaped brooch decorating his chest:

"When you take it off," I hear myself tell him, "you'll be dead."

The secret lights up his flush, shimmery face. Now I know he can do with his life whatever he wants, and that from now on, somehow, we'll be traveling in opposite directions.

"What about you, Harumi?"

I know we both share a sense of curiosity. But I really don't need to prove that I was alive. I settle down into bed and position his metal hands, his hard metallic hands on top of the soft feather pillow, which he'll cover my face with as soon as he knows I'm asleep.

I'm not sure if he'll go through with it.

But in case I wake up and I'm dead, I concentrate on a memory.

On one.

And that voice that carries it still sounds like my own.

Tattooed

1.

PEDRO DE ASSÍS DECIDED it was time to fill the empty spot on his body, following the flare-up of hostilities in São Clemente. That afternoon, he abandoned the home he owned on Rúa Niemeyer to occupy the hillside shack where he was born forty-seven years earlier. *Mamboretá had come back*. The rumor of his reappearance trickled through the city—slowly, stumblingly, persistently, till it crossed the asphalt and the fleet feet of people laden with bad blood and malice took care of the rest. Soon they hushed, only to confirm quickly, "Mamboretá has come back." And in no time his murky depths, the astonishing exactitude of chance that winds through the last cycle of his life's story was etched on the front pages of newspapers, and once settled there, his metaphor subtly received the endorsement it needed to become irrevocable.

And it was war.

***

We had inherited Tomé's businesses a few months earlier. I mean Belego and the rest of the old man's circle, his nephews and second cousins. Suddenly we were gathering out of habit in what used to be his living room, eating his food, following his customs, not really missing him much, or asking anyone's permission. Life went back to normal about three days after the wake, when Belego opened the sealed door and freed the sour air like an exhalation. Everyone preferred to skirt the fact that Tomé had been taken out by seven stab wounds in a São Conrado flophouse. The reasons for his murder—you know it better than anyone—were what sparked the war, stitched so tightly to his corpse that people started whispering and telling stories until Mamboretá showed up and silently confirmed the rumors flying around that Pinheiro was the assassin. There was no question that the old man had been the closest thing to a father the Visitor had ever had; and though we had amassed debts on his account, we knew there was one more Tomé had left behind, and it was on us to deal with it.

It was a Thursday.

The open door grinned like a toothless mouth, and despite the midday brightness that streamed in through the windows, the assembly of black men spread through the workshop in nocturnal circumspection. They took over the place in no time, probing every corner with the geometry of experience. They scrutinized, suspected, and before long fell silent. (Only later did we learn that Pinheiro had put a price on Andorinho that very afternoon, same as he had the old man: hands tied behind his back, stabbed in the abdomen, throat sliced open and drooping like an eyelid over a table covered in newspaper clippings and red papers responding to the threat of return.) We observed it through the lens of suspicion that fed our thinking. But Mamboretá was blond and fearless. His fiery, pale blue eyes commanded authority, and he wielded it with the vertigo of a powerful addiction, something that governed his every gesture, even when dictated from despair, as was the case then. His drug was so strong people happily sacrificed their lives to follow his orders, and later we were able to count and confirm just how many. Whenever he killed an enemy he would hold his solemn, sinewy hands together and say a prayer, as if he felt compunction over his own power.

Taking over the studio, he welcomed the men with nothing but his open hand, and they quit lurking around to settle in and inhabit the space, woven together by a strange web of strategies and superstitions. They peeked out through the blinds, the guards in positions higher up, and though everyone knew nothing would happen, the oldest man in the group—a black man called Cuaresma—insisted that nobody come in or out, and we calmly followed his orders. Mamboretá motioned with his hand held high, and the entire scene froze in place. We remembered Tomé, his wide feline smile that curved up at the corners and that tank top matting the white hairs of his chest, the tangle of gold chains around his neck, gleaming and thick as creepers in a briar patch. How he would have welcomed us same as he always did: with a big bear hug and effusive shows of affection. But Tomé was gone now, and nobody knew how to enact the old ceremony without the bounty of his belly laugh. Mamboretá perched himself on the room's only sofa, as he'd done so many times when we weren't present, and the words Tomé predicted he would utter now slipped from his tongue, perfectly synchronized. It seemed as though old Tomé had never left.

"Someone they call Belego . . ." the Visitor said, finally.

We looked at Milton, in a corner of the room.

Now that we knew, it was on him to seal the old man's prophecy.

"Don't know anything else right now," Mamboretá continued, stretched comfortably on the piece of furniture: he goes by Belego and he was el Viejo's favorite.

Mamboretá no longer doubted it. "Could it be?"

2.

Sliding down to the Copacabana shore in its green-hued skin and exuberant shadow of black kids, São Clemente knew that Mamboretá was who they said he was because nothing defined him better than his own tracks. He had collected many debts and wore each one tattooed on his body like a badge after the battle, even the ones he hadn't fought yet. Maybe that's why he'd never squared up with Pinheiro, an old sector pal whose collections in the southern zone were putting him on edge. Pinheiro soon became an enemy when he secretly located a new supplier from inside Sergipe.

Since the mid-sixties, São Clemente had grown in the way of all beasts: with pure instinct, pure freedom. Once it came of age, there was no use trying to domesticate it. Soon the neighborhood was running wild, the first kites flying over the neighboring favela where many of the uprooted Pernambucans now found a natural passageway to the richest areas of Río. Political authority was limited to men in blue uniforms whose shiny helmets, when seen from above, blended in with the rest of the city: a panoramic view that we alone could see, like the reflection of the ocean itself. Dead laws allowed business to prosper. But the day Mamboretá found out that Pinheiro was taking from him by dealing behind his back, he wanted to devour him like an old god swallows his own son, and the war raged without a truce since Pinheira turned out to be more powerful than anyone had suspected.

Suns and moons came and went, and pestilential insects buzzed through the hillside air. The metallic snarl of gunfire rang out, filling the night with cartridge after cartridge; bullets skimmed flesh and plunged without prejudice into soft human tissue. Many fell. Others rose. They reached agreements. They reneged on them. The war raged for days and months. Nobody realized that the pile of the dead was as tall as the one that now gave us space for life until it occurred to someone to take account. Finally the newspapers began echoing the voices of sensible people, obliging the administration in Planalto to get involved and soon conciliatory rhetoric followed, maybe to avoid being pulled into the muck of blue moles or other squads that blocked the Northeast's prosperous drug trade. In fact, the old leaders began embracing Pinheiro's strategies, refining the ways of doing business. In some house along the Passeio de Tiradentes, bedecked in white shoes and swanky manners, the old men still awarded Mamboretá a few big contracts, but ended up relegating his management to the least important areas of Río. In the splendidness of their power, they had no more than to close their fingers to end the story. This is how they wanted it to go. And this is how it went.

3.

His real name was Milton Menezes, but everyone here goes by whatever name the street gives you. They'd called him Belego since he was a kid. Pedro de Assís had been called Guaraní or Paraguayo, same as his mother when she arrived, a widow who had nothing to her name but the child she carried in her belly. But over time, Mamboretá forged his own name, far removed from Creará where his parents, his dead father, came from; and over time he'd become a man of action, which is just as defining and worthy of respect as the legend that has accompanied him ever since, from the heart of São Clemente.

How about I tell you something now that we have a minute and the story still has a blush in its cheek. His is a grand tale. But let's see . . . where to begin? How about that afternoon he showed up at Tomé's studio and sat back on the sofa to address the black men gathered there: "He was the Misionero's favorite. They call him Belego. May God preserve in his glory the righteous men of our land." Yes: *Mamboretá had come back*. The black men, crossing themselves same as he did, looked solemn and downcast, as was customary when showing respect for the dead. We saw them shaking each other's hands vigorously, as if they'd known each other forever. And then, abruptly, Mamboretá's mood perked up and he told them to fetch some weed so we could smoke while Belego was tattooing his body. We thanked him. It was a modest studio and we didn't want to get in the way. The light filtered through hungrily, licking the windows, and the distant murmur of *barrio medio's* parade seemed to ask permission before entering, browbeaten and self-effacing. Nevertheless, Belego led Mamboretá to his corner behind the folding screen and set to work. Every once in a while we could hear the Visitor's voice through the flimsy partition, a voice unwinding like a great skein of wool, falling over us like Venetian blinds in the middle of the afternoon. Belego kept quiet. And we kept quiet too, imagining him pulling the stencil from a drawer and showing it to Mamboretá, because soon we heard him say "beautiful" and we knew he'd only pronounce the word when he saw the tattoo the old man had bequeathed. He traced the stencil on Mamboretá's chest, the only spot that for fifteen years Tomé had left free for Belego could fill it in now.

The needle skipped into motion. The unmistakable sound of the insect at work.

"Did he ever explain why that space was left blank?"

The black men smoked and made a racket, like a pack of crows: we listened in the distance, from our circle of weed.

Mamboretá said, "No, he didn't. I had wanted to tattoo it in the fifth time we met. It seemed spooky to leave a blank white spot over my heart like that, like an invitation for death. But each time I came back over the following months, the old man refused. I finally insisted again a year later. He didn't even bother to answer me. But he wasn't being rude, I knew him enough to figure he had his reasons, I was just curious to know what he intended. So I asked who was going to do it if not him. "Belego," he said. The name sounded familiar to me. My mother and I heard him mention that name once, back when the old man came to our house every day to preach the gospel, when São Clemente was no more than a tiny group of shacks patched together with caravan parts left by people who had just arrived from the Creará coast or from Bahia. He made the story sound like an old parable, like one of those religious stories he used to teach us that imitated things so important back in their time, but now gasped comically outside what we understood to be true. So I asked flippantly: "Since when have you become superstitious, old man?" "The day I tattooed a dead man," he answered. I doubted. And he added quickly: "Only the dead can't die." The thought didn't bother me that much, but still I said to him: "You take risks running your mouth like that. One of these days someone's going to shut it up the wrong way." He laughed then, I remember. But Christ our Savior, who rests in God's glory, had heard me.

A faint, rustling murmur kicked up outside. The festival gestated discreetly on the other side of the walls, the clapboard beams, the little piles of trash, while the city's emblematic sites looked out at us from the distance and smiled, triumphant. Today the *mid-barrio* celebrates its new year, we remembered, and the procession would make its way down towards Copacabana along a zigzagging route that represents the wild path men must take to reach the kingdom of Yemanja: women shimmy under the weight of their plumage and oils, their white linen dresses, the tambourines and drums giving shape to their clay bodies, sculptors committed to perfection. What other forms of paradise could be found in the dark sensuality, the swelling that came in wave after wave, arching and agile, that finally regrouped in a seaside celebration? The sun glimmered in through the lace curtains, winking at us in sly, delicate nods, making sure we didn't miss the signs of the things we didn't know how to see. We barely paid attention to what Mamboretá was saying with clairvoyant vision.

"When something ends, you must be prepared to start over again."

Belego moved his face away from the window, where certain bodies were beginning to look real in the filthy haze. The sound was still hard to distinguish; it came in slices, as if by knife strokes. The day, like a shredded rag along the horizon, became some other place.

"That's what Tomé said," he finished.

But in his silence, Belego already new that.

The old man had been repeating the same words to him his entire life.

4.

There are times when I see not one, but several signs in what I'm doing. It's not like working on paper that you can toss in the trash when the design is flawed or has lost its allure. Not like love or fear. Not as profound as guilt, though the mark, inked onto the skin forever, acquires a peculiar strength that roots so deeply it becomes part of your identity. If not, you'd never have selected it to accompany you till the day you die, which is the end of existence, of substance. End of the road. You're a mile lost in the middle of the goddamn desert. It's irrevocable, like death in all its forms, and it's good that it be this way, we respect life all the more deeply because we're conscious of its irreversible nature. That's how to think of it. As the only thing you can be one hundred percent sure will stay with you forever. Not a lover, not a wife, not a brother; no happy memory; no friendly, familiar image. It's just you and the tattoo, invited to the spectacle of your last, stumbling breath. What can be better than that? What can be better than watching this potential spectacle, like others watch a mother giving birth to a new life? Surely there's got to be something. Once the scab has fallen off, it will never miss a date: you'll look at your arm and there it is; it'll wave goodbye and then what? Your skin will be covered in new marks, furrows, wrinkles and tints, it will be devoured by time, which corrupts everything, and return once again to the cloth rag from which our artisan takes all the skins that clothe men and women on Earth. Only hatred, really, holds a similar brand of ink, so murky and categorical. But it doesn't last either: before the moment of death all people are righteous, nobody spares a kind word, or big-hearted epigraph, tears or a fond memory. It's the written map of your life. What else gives a similar sense of power? Murder. Yes, killing someone else. The only thing on par with tattooing someone's body: killing someone. Just hold that thought for a minute. Who wants a stigma seeping so far into the body, mooring itself so deeply as to plumb the depths of your own conscience? The only mark that will be with you the day you breathe your last breath and hang up your skin before sinking into the immaterial, the mark that will observe you, and remain in the place you gave it in the world. It will say goodbye from the distance, and it's good that that's

the way it is. Choice always brings the same measure of account-
ability, the same wisdom: that from silence, you too have brought
something of importance along with you.

5.

Mamboretá is curious, "Have you ever been in prison,
Belego?"

The question doesn't seem to surprise him, though the
Visitor's tone of voice does. There's nothing confidential
binding them, but there's an air of complicity. Though
somewhat stiff, the look in Pedro de Assís's eyes expresses
something serene and unassuming, which has a calming effect. Belego is holding the answer between his left
thumb and index finger, motionless: a seven-figure tattoo
stencil that anyone who has been to Araraquara could
easily interpret. His question seems awkward now, sec-
ondary, and even redundant. Yet Belego keeps focused
on the needlework, his answer requires no embellishment
or patience, and he understands the question as being
some coarse form of courtesy.

"Yes," he replies. "A long time ago, in São Paulo," he
explains, "it was a petty allegation. Could've been jealou-
sy, maybe. I never found out. God knows, ain't no justice
for poor folk, but I got through it thanks to the protection
of someone as great as him."

And he dares to ask: "What about you, sir?"

Nestled like a whale on sand, Mamboretá opens his
wide mouth full of molars and a there's a sudden twinkle

from the slice of gold fitted between his right canine and front teeth. Yet the vulgar gleam of his teeth only serves to depreciate his expression, exposing a scarred network of feelings as tangled and dark as the tribal designs tattooed across his forearms.

Eventually, his smile shuts like a trap.

"Yes," he says. "For murder."

"Murder," the other repeats.

"Yep, murder . . ." the Visitor says. "Murder."

He laughs for no apparent reason. "And you?"

Belego pauses, moves the needle away from Pedro de Assis's skin and sets it down beside the ink.

An elusive film seems to smear across his eyes.

"Well . . ." he begins.

He had pronounced these same words a thousand times trying to imagine the situation; a thousand times copying his voice, a thousand times betting on how the first person to know his sin would react, what expression would show on their face. And yet the only word that escaped him every time was simple. "Fraud," he would say. Brief, though fitting proof that what he'd done was behind him now, and he was at peace with his past. But with Mamboretá on the receiving end of his confession, Belego realizes how insignificant the crime is. His voice quivers, as if suddenly he were completely drained of self-confidence.

"Something like that," he says after a while.

The Visitor slaps his thighs vehemently.

"Something like that?" he says. "You fucking with me? Far as I know in this life, either you kill a man or you don't. No something 'like' killing a man. You do it when the time comes, right?" he stops. "So, what you got to say?"

He lets it go. "There're lots of ways of killing a man, sir. Worst may be by saving him."

6.

It took a few decades for the others to propagate, spreading over his body like the roots of a tree. Now this was the only empty patch left, just beside his sternum. Every inch of him was covered; his forearms with black tribal marks and Biblical scenes—the crucifixion and the miracle of the water springing in the desert—his stomach and back were wreathed with Japanese demons, everything in its place for a reason, imbued with a meaning, and he was like a transparent book that allowed him to read himself through the old man's eyes, how the old man had abandoned his missionary faith to become a sedentary tattoo artist in a São Clemente hovel. There were black fish in an *irezumi*, and a few *kanji* characters that the Visitor translated as an old-fashioned show of sentimental nationalism: *Ordem e progresso*. There was a woman's profile and her dreamy smile, a clock without hands, and a leopard pouncing from among tall grass, wild as the Guarani blood his mother spilled in childbirth.

Belego could imagine the illustrations continuing down

his thigh, sliding inside his pant leg and continuing the tale. Rocha must certainly be somewhere in the mix, the sergeant who had been gunned down in Vidigal when his negotiations with a new Pernambuco distributor were uncovered. Or Emerson and Queiroz, who tried to start up a new gang, the Comando Vermelho, aborted three weeks before it was born when the members were left on the asphalt eighteen rounds later. Fifteen years was a long time.

Belego turned the machine on and made himself comfortable. "When something ends, you must be prepared to start over," he said. The time had come to begin anew. But this case went beyond beginning and ending; it went far beyond ending and beginning again. This had to do with reaching the end of the line, the map of an entire life, a cycle that was finally coming to a close. *Does he understand that?* Every end is a new beginning, he said to himself. And though it wasn't an original idea, at least by witnessing the abundance of that other skin, his actions gained coherence now, with his words and memories.

Belego signaled to the cot and Mamboretá lay down, not without first reminding Belego of Tomé's promise, which was now his by inheritance.

"You got it?" Mamboretá asked before reclining further, referring to the orchid.

"I do."

Belego went to fetch the stencil from the drawer where he kept it safe, shuffling around in the papers. He didn't want Mamboretá to see it, knowing he wouldn't understand its form or significance until it was nestled into its proper space in the map of his body. He finished the work in no time, and when he peeled the paper away from his chest, the purple ink left a visible trace of what he would now go to work on with the needle and a steady pulse.

Mamboretá looked at the shape in the mirror.

"Beautiful," he said.

Yes, it was *beautiful*.

"Just like he said it would be."

Mamboretá settled in a little more, but there was still something else he wanted to know.

"I didn't ask before out of respect for the old man."

"What is it?"

"How old are you?"

"Nineteen," Belego said.

Mamboretá nodded: it was clear that the old man had broken his vow of chastity years before he'd set up in São Clemente.

"You look like him," was all he said. "Even more now that I can see in you the things he no longer had." He closed his eyes and leaned back on the soft oyster of fabric, and didn't move again, "Go ahead, let's do this."

Sure, he thought. Let's get started. We're all just a long stretch of miles lost in the goddamn desert.

As the festival played on outside, the machine did its job. Quick pricks of the needle stained his skin, injecting the ink like black poison.

The insect hovered over his chest alone for a few minutes.

Listening closely, under the Visitor's rough skin, you could hear a slight electric pulse. Yep: there was the beat of a tiny heart.

7.

One of the black men talked about Tomé, about him preaching the word of Christ our Savior till he lost his faith, how the old man had wandered the deserts of clairvoyance. They talked about African ancestors and magic. Faith was an important thing, they said. Forgiveness is the beginning of faith, and faith the end of all searching.

"One of these days," we hear the youngest of the four speak out, raising his voice above the others, "I'm going to leap from this window, ten stories down, and I ain't gonna die. Listen up, citizen. I will leap and I will walk to the bench down yonder, and I will go and walk all the way home. Won't be no night, won't be no sad day. Day's gonna come when I have faith in myself, I will leap and it will be a day of illumination. There will be light. Light in all places, in every eye, in every spirit. Listen up, because it will be the day of my triumph. There are two kinds of people in this world. People who leap without faith in themselves, and who die in the void, and people whose faith sustains them, who fall on their feet and walk away. Our Lord and Savior Jesus Christ walked on the waters of the ocean, over temptation, over the muck of death, and he did not sink into the void or the darkness, because he only had faith in himself; He already lost hope in others and His faith alone is what protected Him. Those who are like Him don't care what other people say, people try to defeat them, to discourage them, to finish them off. If you have faith in yourself, my brother, how can you die?"

Out of curiosity, we tried to locate the origin of the voice, hoping to encounter some entity dissolving into the late afternoon, but instead we saw just another body, like any other.

After a while, Belego looked up and gazed over the screen. Only Cuaresma was allowed to cross the space separating the boss from the rest of them, and he disappeared behind the old fabric as if under the wing of a giant bird. We could hear him praising the tattoo, and so we approached cautiously, inquisitively. Mamboretá had only ever allowed the old man to witness the part of the procedure that caused pain, and out of privacy, the old man used to vacate the shop whenever Mamboretá arrived. But that part was over now, and there was nothing to fear. Two and a half hours later, Belego filled in the last strokes. He looked out over his eyeglasses and sponged away the last drops of leftover ink that fell from the needle like tears through thick mascara. *In this profession, any gaffe leaves a mark of imperfection: like moles or scars left by a guilty god. There's someone to curse, to remember with disgust, to blame for faults, unlike the flaws and blemishes given at birth, the result of impersonal and anonymous gods who won't be held ac-*

countable for their work. The skin was still inflamed from the metal abrasion, but the stencil, the greenish-purple stain, emerged through the inflammation. The orchid revealed its difficult beauty, its hidden meanings, and Mamboretá was moved to smiling in a way that made us think he really could decipher its meaning.

He smiled, more than anything.

And tilted his face upwards.

He showed off the mark brazenly, inoffensively, the one so many men have carried as their last memory of this world, that blend of satisfaction and lust that now, as he spoke, was only satisfaction.

"I waited fifteen years to fill this in," he said, "but I never knew this is what it would look like till now."

He touched his chest just above the sternum and patted the boy on the back saying, "Good job, Belego."

Milton extended his hand, now free of the surgeon's gloves that lay sloughed like another skin on top of the table. Freed of his debt, he was like a reptile that shed vestiges of his own personality. A tail, a few scales. After they left, a watery, black and gray orchid with shadows and shades of red, planted itself forever on the body of a dead man.

That's what they say. Orchids can have everlasting lives, because they live as long as the tree that gives them shelter.

He left the Visitor scrutinizing himself in the mirror, and poured some water into two glasses.

He came back with them, filled to the brim.

"Drink up," he said.

They looked at each other and didn't hesitate, drinking at the same time.

"Now that you have an orchid on your body," he said, taking back the empty glass, "Don't forget to water it."

Mamboretá nodded, raising himself slowly from the cot.

"I'll keep it in mind," he said. "We should say a prayer now for Tomé."

He put his long, spindly hands together and closed his eyes.

Beside him, Belego bowed his head reverently, to show respect.

We did the same.

"Our Lord Jesus Christ," his voice rose and waned like an old heartbeat, "who art in Heaven, preserve those who profess your Kingdom in the world of men, as unto your hands may the spirit of Tomé be laid to rest, an upright counselor, loyal friend, that we may pronounce the bounty of Thy name, and Tomé avail himself of nothing other than Your strength when the way is prepared for Your coming in the fight against sin. Deliver me from the evil that is inside of me, and in others. Amen."

"Amen," the black men repeated outside.

"Amen," we said.

Mamboretá smoothed his hair back with his hands. We applied a scarring unguent and moisturizer to his chest, and covered it with transparent gauze. He slipped his shirt back on and gathered his things to leave, talking about the old man again, how good he had been.

"He was decent," he said, closing his hand slightly now, in retreat.

"You're lucky to have had a father like him."

He buttoned his shirt, and was gone just a minute later.

We could hear the car drive away before closing the window.

Inside, Cuaresma had left a big wad of bills on the sofa. The bills were spread on top of the envelope, like an ear of corn, but we hardly bothered to count them.

Deep down we were embarrassed.

8.

Specks of light like teeth marks on skin. Bare backs, sprightly glimmers, shivering plumages as if the Earth had suddenly bowed in their celebration. A heartbeat: Boom! Boom! The drum procession, driving forward unpropitious, is the last sign they observe before parking the car along a prohibited zone of the sidewalk. Mamboretá had ordered them to stop a little while earlier, when the first spasms began turning his stomach. Standing still a few meters away from the car, he retched beside a lamppost, vomiting so violently he couldn't tell if he was finished yet. An endless stream of people made their way from the middle *barrio*, dancing, twirling, and dancing. Festive devil masks, exposed skin oiled with a peculiar silvery shimmer, on a relentless journey towards the sea.

The group of black men, protecting their boss, hovers together on the sidewalk, hands over their guns, but here
comes a man decked in a spray of feathers addressing
them, and one of the men jeers at him and the others
soon follow suit. The youngest one volunteers something
about how the fire will rain down upon the kingdoms of
the earth, but his companions meet his comments with
indifference and he soon shuts up. "Oh, Jesus Lord."
Rowdy music accompanies the sparkling procession as
it advances, drums throbbing like a clandestine heart.
Heading down to Leme?, they shout. The plumed man
distracts them, shaking his bare, smooth-shaven ass and
catcalling, "Here." Boom! Boom! as he spanks his ass like
a tambourine and the black men hoot raucously, and
in their excitement fail to see the hands that pull out an
iron beast nearly as powerful as the ones they're carrying.
From among the ribbons of color and pandemonium in
the specter of twilight, a palliative comes whirring, slicing a path through the spirits of the air to ease Mamboretá's malaise as he bends over the sidewalk. Mamboretá
is aware that the death rattles are not fireworks; he knows
they are envoys of a different carnival. It's too late. A perfect hole is sketched on his abdomen, and he concedes
that the perforation is so clean it's an invitation he has no
choice but to accept. Who's to blame? Soon his back pops
like an overinflated balloon; the pain can hardly resist the
skilled messenger now continuing its trajectory towards
the sea. He squints his eyes, lagging before the sudden-

ness of the confusion, the bullet escapes his body, the rush of free air, feeling the absolute outside. And there come other sounds. Broken glass. Muffled metal snaps. The car escapes and in the distance, the procession continues partying on its way to Leme, sliding downhill like a gleaming river of red that feeds the sun. It flickers. It wanes. And disappears. Mamboretá, great as he was, allows himself but a single whim before dying: the asphalt becomes soft as a cushion, and there, looking up at the white sphere which stares down like a huge Cyclops, he will not get up again. *Blessed are those who love for theirs is the kingdom of heaven.* I think that's what he would have said. That his faith, despite everything, would remain intact. And his eyes closed like a trap door that will hold him captive for centuries and centuries, amen.

The plumed man looked down from above, hard-faced, his head eclipsing the sun.

"Is he dead?" the other one asked.

"Don't know," he answered, the revolver still hot in his hands.

He took aim at Mamboretá's forehead and looked away before it exploded and the smell of ash became tangible.

"He's dead now," he said.

The next day, there was graffiti on the wall. A strange drawing, like an open flower, just a few yards from a stain on the sidewalk that was turning black. *Pinheiro rules*, it said. The orchid, like the one on Mamboretá's chest, had opened its petals and bloomed into the intense red of a kiss. That's what we heard, anyway. Someone saw Belego leave shortly afterwards, on the road to São Clemente, and Pinheiro showed up, and other than the seven numbers tattooed on his hands, Belego never wore a mark that wasn't given to him by life itself. I don't know if that's what really happened, but it's what's gone around and that's enough for me. My silence, and the silence of the others, too, is what the ancients choose, and they say it didn't take long for the first comet to appear in the sky that afternoon.

It was the first sign of our reconciliation.

The Island

For my parents, who invited me on this journey.

1.

THE DAY HAD BEEN SO CRISP and clear that Guilherme remembers that afternoon particularly well. A small boat
carved ripples in front of the island. Capitán Nemo was
driving, and Guilherme's father, Luizinho, waited for just
the right moment to disappear. Isn't that what he'd always done when at the sea's indefinite edge? Submerge,
disappear? But something held him back that afternoon.
Guilherme thinks back on it now that the sea's wrinkled
forehead observes him, glimmering without animosity,
like a beast tamed over time.

A few yards away, in the exact spot where his memory
had left off, the sand-hued belly of a great fish appears
from the aquatic depths, and its meaning, which continues hidden today as it was then, acquires significance in
his life. It was no longer the silvery creature that fights,
tail thrashing to and fro against the glistening line, or that
species of wrath tangled up in the nets, but something
that smolders quietly and burns out in the heat of the sun-
stricken afternoon. It became the image of death, floating belly up and white as the sun seen head on, nothing

that had come as it had before by the effort of his arms, or pulling a fish hook from gasping jaws struggling to breathe out of the water. It came just like that, unexpectedly. Silently, like a bubble exhaled. The fish was lulled by an overly gentle movement, even for a dead creature. Steady in the bow, Guiraldes assured us it was about the strangest thing he'd ever seen. And Luizinho, looking puzzled, swore it was true.

Guiraldes often joined them on their excursions to the city in that big black car with leather seats and power windows. The truth was Luizinho would never go to the island without that giant, with his colossal arms and smile, with whom he shared a special bond. Once in a while his father would dive in, and he'd watch his arms stroking the water, how he'd dry himself off when he reached the sandy shore; there were times he'd stay on the island for hours. He doesn't mind remembering it this way: spending time alone with Guiraldes in the boat, getting to know him better, his stories of the high seas, calling him Capitán Nemo after something he'd read in school. He would always be Capitán Nemo to him from then on. No matter how deeply he explores his memory, Guiraldes always obeyed Luizinho whenever he pointed to the island, and the motor's racket drowned out what the men were shouting to each other at the bow: his father's voice giving the final order before he disappeared. That's why it came as no surprise to Guilherme that while the brink of Capitán Nemo's skiff cut through the water that afternoon, Guiraldes reacted in full compliance, rowing quietly towards the fish, or that Luizinho would stretch out a long arm to bring the dripping animal he snared a few seconds before in the belly of his net. Once he'd gotten his balance again, he laid the catch on a plank beside the basket and patiently cleaned the scales and gutted it, slicing what was left into several regular pieces.

"We have bait for a half hour's fishing," Luizinho said.

And as if that serene understanding of life wasn't enough, Capitán Nemo added, "It was just an old fish."

The catch wasn't good that afternoon, they had to throw a few eels back in and Luizinho, who was back before long from his excursion to the island, had to admit that using bait the ocean had spit out might not have been a good idea. "The sea doesn't want what it's already expelled." A new wrinkle showed up in his face that afternoon, barely noticeable under the film of water he didn't bother to dry off when he hopped back onboard. He surveyed the day's catch in silence, and said nothing more until finally ordering Guiraldes to pull the chord, turning the motor over with an oily snarl.

When they were far enough away that the island appeared the size of something that could be trapped between his fingers, his countenance relaxed and his body was now dry.

He spent the rest of the afternoon with a sad smile on

his face, and a dark mood that Guilherme had noticed immediately, not prompted by words drowned out by the motor or by the air or even the boat's soporific rocking as it carried them home. As far as he could recall it came from a certain grimace that Capitán Nemo placated through camaraderie, but also with a veiled sense of discomfort.

So long afterwards, and Guilherme still remembers his own disquiet, but for different reasons.

He didn't catch a thing that afternoon in front of the island.

2.

Dad was taken away six hours ago. They had a hard time fitting him into the box they used to ship him off to the cemetery. He'd gained so much weight over the past few years that it was difficult to find a proper suit that would fit. He'd always been so dignified and elegant and he deserved to bid farewell to life in the same honorable fashion he'd come in. The bureaucracy of death always exceeds our own faculty for suffering, I thought, while the mortuary affairs kept me on the outside of what was taking place. By the end of the day, this was the only conclusion I felt like drawing. Life imagines us, and suddenly any old day becomes today; you look in the mirror, you sit at the table, you open the family album and know perfectly well that someone saw you crying; you listen attentively to the person who is telling you about it, feeling a bit skeptical, as if they were making up a fairy tale full of contradictions. Death, on the other hand, obliges us to imagine it as something severe and yet condescending, like an old governess chock-full of virtues that take a long time to finally appreciate. We all bring the same secret with us in the end, the same one we had desperately hoped someone else would share: will we ever see each other again?

At the end of a long day of insurance policies and payments in places that show their sympathy according to the size of one's bank account, Luizinho's death, my father's, was exactly what it was, not the funereal greasepaint of commitments and formalities, not the absurd and evasive fulfilling of tasks. It was no more than his death, that cold expediency through which I could channel the best of his own way of approaching things, which is to say, by working. Finally standing alone before the coffin I'd helped close four hours earlier, exhausted and overwhelmed by my own efforts, I was finally able to cry.

As dusk fell, the others began to arrive; people I was familiar with and recognized, that I knew had known him. They all spoke kind words. They shook my hand. Told me how sorry they were. They understood, as I had, that his death had suddenly aged them all. Without my realizing it, most of the place was filled with men his own age, men who today would have colleagues or childhood friends who had died before he did. I had grateful words for all of them and showed my appreciation, as did my wife and son when they were required, their indirect pain subjecting them to a strange test of loyalty. It had been easier for them to relieve their sadness than for me, and aware of their strength, I left them in the parlor and went out into the vestibule that lead outside, looking for an empty seat and perhaps a little comfort.

People were gathered around the door smoking when someone walked through them with difficulty, aided by a metal cane. There he was, five years later, João Guiraldes. I had been away for four years, and the last summer Dad spent out of the hospital, he decided he could get along without him, that João was getting old and needed to rest (they both needed to rest he said). I never gathered the nerve to visit him in the infirmary where he was living, shut in by cataracts that were getting bluer and bluer as the days went by. I could already see from the short distance that separated us that he was somewhat disoriented, which I attributed to grief. It was the first time I'd ever seen him lose the perfect equilibrium he'd learned in my father's service.

I approached him.

"Capitán Nemo," I said.

João Guiraldes looked unsurprised, and only then did I realize he'd gone blind. His eyes, fixed on me, were lacquered with a milky film whose color was reminiscent of aquatic reflections. It brought to mind the eyes of fish outside the water: the kind that stare at us, pierced by the sun.

"Guilhe . . ." he said, instinctively. I watched the rough

tenderness in his face stirred by subtle emotion: "I'm so sorry about your father, my boy. I found out this afternoon and came as soon as I could . . ."

"I appreciate it," I interrupted, not wanting to hear his condolences. "You have as much right to be here as I do, you know."

He shook his head, but I held his arm caringly and thanked him again. It was strange to realize that now I was bigger and stronger than him, though I'd grown up beside him and spent most of my life admiring his oak-like burliness. His arm felt like a vase in my hand, something I was afraid of damaging. So I insisted. I could have said it all night long because it was the truth, because he deserved it, because without a doubt my father would have wanted me to. I led him to a seat in the hallway and helped him to sit down. I took his cane and rested it against the wall.

"Your father was a good man," he said after a while, when I was at a loss for what else to ask about his life.

I was now aware that he had retired, that he lived in a pleasant assisted living facility where the nurses no longer felt the need to encourage his self-reliance or desire to feel young and useful anymore.

"But they're nice people," he smiled, without malice, pointing to the exit door. "In fact, one of the nurses came with me today. She's waiting outside. Don't judge her too quickly. She's big-hearted with me and takes care of me more than she should."

I smiled and saw that he could tell. I didn't look through the glass.

"I'm a poor old man without eyes, but I can see things clearly," he sighed. "Do you know what I mean? If it weren't for your father I'd be asking for handouts on some dark street corner, or dead, run over by someone in a hurry or by my own hand, someone who couldn't see to stop or go in time . . . A man whose only gift is strength, without eyes, is nothing but a nuisance to the rest of his body . . . But your father, my boy . . ."

I wanted to tell him that maybe he wouldn't have gone blind if he hadn't worked for my father, but there was no reason to ruin the image he had of him for some stupid rhetorical exercise. After all, he'd never have the chance to see him other ways. It was true that my father had helped him more than anyone else had, maybe better than anyone, and that's certainly worth something to someone who had nothing but gratitude.

An uncomfortable silence fell between us, but Guiraldes restrained himself and didn't cry. For some reason I began to wonder whether the blind were able to cry, until the shadowy frou-frou of taffeta and ruffles cast its length over us, and when I looked up there she was. Before I saw her standing between us, Guiraldes had already greeted his nurse.

"Daniela," he said, raising his voice a touch, "This is Guilherme . . ."

The woman, a gaunt, aseptic figure, extended her hand and touched my shoulder. "My sympathies, Mr. Fonseca."

"Mister Fonseca . . ." I repeated, measuring my words. I felt as though she were talking to my father and thanked her out of inertia, but there was something about the scene that seemed unacceptable to me, and I wasn't able to hold her gaze, look her in the eye, I couldn't abide her white nylons, let alone those immaculate, sanitized shoes. The way her eyes took me in, pierced me and penetrated deep inside like no other person in the room, it was too potent to share with anyone else. I couldn't bear it, I didn't want to bear it, but even still I said thank you anyway. I expressed my gratitude, as the real Mr. Fonseca would have done. It was my duty to be understanding and offer kind words.

I tore my eyes from her skirt and stood up.

She was a tall woman.

"Thanks for being here," I said hurriedly.

"Sure," Guiraldes said, trying to get to his feet.

The nurse and I helped him up; we handed him his cane and he stood there stiff and unsteady.

"I'm going to offer my condolences to the rest of the family," he said, finally finding his words.

"I'll accompany you, sir."

I knew he'd never get used to being treated that way: he, who'd always been on the other side. I took him by the arm and we walked to the coffin. I imagined it would be a useless venture since he wouldn't be able to see him; but he was so adamant on getting there and in expressing his sympathies to my wife and young son that I couldn't refuse. When we were finally beside my dead father, I could feel Guiraldes squeeze my arm tighter and his heart starting beating faster.

"The body's swollen," he whispered.

I didn't know—and didn't dare ask—if he was addressing me or himself, or maybe even my father. I looked at him with curiosity and saw that he was trembling. He was overwhelmed with emotion but knew he was being observed, so he made the sign of the cross and asked to be taken away. People watched us pass on our way to the hall and its empty seats, people still hovered around the threshold smoking, as if in the meantime we'd never gone anywhere. I delivered him to the nurse again, this old man who had taken such good care of me, whom I loved so much, and the nurse seemed mindful of how much this simple act meant to both of us. Guiraldes, Capitán Nemo, hugged me when we said goodbye and his breath, as bitter and inevitable as old age, filled my ear.

"Would you like to get to know the island?" he said.

"What?" I answered.

"Get to know it . . . what's there beyond the shore, on land. Want to see it?"

3.

Luizinho never wanted to have a child. Truth is he'd never actually had time to think about having one until the afternoon Nuria surprised him with the news of her pregnancy. Nuria might not have wanted one either, but her docile, lackadaisical nature made her more amenable to the situation, and in the end it was her vitality before the inevitable arrival of motherhood that ended up encouraging her boyfriend and future husband. Nine months later, Luizinho became a father. His son came to this world in splendid health, yawping heartily from the maternity ward till he went purple. Deeply touched by the experience, his father gave him the name of Guilherme in memory of his paternal grandfather, a Portuguese merchant who greeted him with shouts every time he caught sight of him along the old docks.

Luizinho left his college studies five months later, promising himself he'd go back a little later on. He started working in his father's store, a prosperous food import bazaar where he started as assistant accountant and moved up the ranks until he was finally named the managing director. Two years later, when Luiz senior—precipitated by diabetes and failing health—decided to retire and leave the company in his son's hands, Luizinho considered that experience had taught him all he needed to know about business and the idea of going back to college was filed away as something he'd never really missed out on. Nuria was a conventional, though sweet-natured wife. And with Guilherme, who kept growing bigger and stronger, the future now smiled at him with the cutest little dimples and a whole new perspective on life. The serene life cycle before him, which he'd have to finish on his own, was a promise he'd accepted without misgivings or substitutes. He understood it as characteristic adulthood, which came with the heavy feet of habit, silent and patient, and time softened as a result, choosing its own rhythm and form.

But illness arrived.

One afternoon the doctors referred them to a specialist in the city so that Nuria could receive some explanation for the pain in her lower abdomen. Luizinho was twenty-five years old, and could tell right away they'd never go back to the way they'd been before they left. He remembers sleeping in the hotel that night, something they hadn't even done after their hasty, spare wedding, but Nuria was able to sleep comfortably, not for his embraces, but thanks to the tranquilizer that hypnotized away her pain.

The hospital was a big, cold building at the end of a frenzied avenue. Miraculously, the noise didn't reach it. He waited in the hallway, a long throat of blanched white tiles, until one of the nurses finally gave him the go-ahead he'd been kept waiting for. The doctors were up front with him and he was grateful to them for it. They said the uterus had never recovered from a natural tear, probably the result of childbirth, and it usually happened when a child was born beyond the due date, as was the case with his son, exacerbated by the fact that the mother's body was too small. Cancer, the doctor explained, before underscoring the fact that the tumor had taken root in her body, metastasizing, and there was nothing to be done except radiation.

That night, Nuria said that perhaps she was never meant to have a child, that she was too petite for giving birth, as her grandmother had warned; but that it was her sacrifice, and in a sense, one life had been given for another. Luizinho remembers how he cried when she finally fell asleep, because he imagined she would never wake up again, and when she died two months later, he had almost believed her dead already, as if her last spasm took a mere shell, intact only by willpower fueled by the little desire she had to remain.

The priest read a Psalms on the day of the funeral, his voice cooing through little Guilherme's hair, whose head lay on the shoulder of an ancient aunt accustomed to protocols of compassion and comfort. Afterwards, Luizinho thanked the priest, kissed his son, and drove around town until the car ran out of gas.

When people ask Guilherme if he remembers his mother, he always says no. But sometimes he feels as though he were lying, as kids do when they're up to mischief. And when he blows out the candles on a birthday cake he feels a pang of guilt, aware that he's also celebrating his mother's death. In many ways, his father had been everything to him. And though he missed his company at times—something he valued precisely because of it being so rare—he feels his father's respect and admiration, and he was always there when he needed his support. What Guilherme would never know is that his mother enjoyed very little of Luizinho's industriousness, which became the curative for his sorrow, and to which he applied such exceptional tenacity that he became the town's wealthiest citizen.

Guilherme remembers him tall and elegant, with that air of premature prosperity, saying goodbye on a field trip to the wetlands, or the first day of school, or a visit to the dentist or the first time he took him to the island. He had already met Capitán Nemo—though he called him Guiraldes—he was the one who brought him to and from school, crossing the town's green fields till the suburbs appeared and then again when they reached a hillock covered in robust, straight-backed pine trees, and then the brick wall appeared, enclosing the category of place that Luizinho had always wanted for his only son's education.

Every time he asked why they stayed back in the skiff alone while his father swam to the island, he always said that he would understand one day when he got older. But he stopped caring to know when he got older, and he stopped asking the question. As a boy it made him joyful to watch how his father's head emerged from the foam. One New Year's spent by the boat, he was in good spirits because the fishing had been bountiful that afternoon and everything went back to normal when Capitán

Nemo raised anchor and they returned to the beach. The car. The foliage. The pale brick wall. A black woman who was a mean cook prepared the meals for my father's weekend parties with his friends; tall, sophisticated men like him, their endless laughter keeping him company as he slept.

Luizinho never remarried. When asked, years later, he said it was because nobody could ever make him forget his mother; that sometimes it's better to die than not to die entirely. Watching him move into the distance, out there on the shore, a chunk of land bulging up from the ocean like giant's knee, Guilherme would consider how tiny his father appeared, and contradiction would enter his life again. Then he'd fish, holding himself in place over the sea, distorting his reflection with a fingertip, fighting the impulse that rose from below. He'd observe how Capitán Nemo would destroy the fishes' mouths to recover the hooks, how they'd curl their bodies in the basket and how he subjugated them with tender, protective force by hitting them against a plank till they were still.

Now, when he thinks back on that time, he admits how his dreams had never been deeper when they got back to land. He misses that sense of peace, though at times, looking at his wife breathing by his side, he believes he's a happy man. Many times he also forgets, he closes his eyes and falls into a deep sleep.

4.

My father and I are together, one summer forty-five years ago. I see him again over me, and he's the same tall cowboy with a checked shirt and cream-colored pants that I put to rest two weeks ago, not as tall, and not as much of a cowboy. His hair is not gray, but black as the frames of his glasses and when he speaks the noise of the motor grinds his words; but I know he's saying something about the island because he's pointing his finger and the other one nods, the sun-dried man that's nodding is Joao Guiraldes, always Capitán Nemo.

I watch the line pulled tight, the luminous wet thread so taut it slices the sea's foam like the sharpest blade. I know the shore is just a few miles away, the structures built in the clear sand that forms dunes and little bulges; beyond that are hedges that contain the desert's relentless incursion like a prehistoric animal straining beneath the weight of its exhausted haunches, brought to its knees by sun and solitude.

What does it matter if I look back again now and find in our starting place nothing more than tiny houses that disappear in a flash, umbrellas opened like the gills of a great fish breathing hidden in the jaws of a wave coming to swallow it. A few children ride crocodiles and tires float a mile in like shipwrecks held by miraculous buoys. The sea abides. Its tongues. Its meanings. We feel its embrace, its phosphorescence under the vigorous March sun, the dashing waves beating against the prow, how they lift us up and free us. But the motor recovers from its time of rest and Capitán Nemo pulls the chord, the propellers grind, the old, heated oil bubbles back and takes the route over. My father smiles and I know the sun is reflected in his glasses, the boat rules the waves with an old sailor at the prow and a fat pelican, mouth agape, devours the wind that challenges our old craft, his old craft on its way to the open sea, charting a singular path diverging from the rest. I know the real reason he's smiling is so I won't be afraid. And that Capitán Nemo understands, the same way he understood my father his entire life.

We continue on toward the island. I see my father signaling ahead and close my eyes, blinded by the sun, and allow myself to be guided at his back, I allow myself to be lulled by the feminine sea and the warm, everlasting tide. It will be our journey to the edge, our confederacy, what pulls us to navigate until the seagulls caw in the opposite direction, then there's no way back and my only desire among so much sea is for more sea and for these revelations to be its most seductive melodies, the sagest echoes of Sirens who've lost their way in time.

"Almost there," Capitán Nemo says, looking at me across his own private sea when I open my eyes.

It's true the island is drawing ever closer and I smile as I place the tiller in his hands and smile at him, like my father did to me when we made this same journey the first time and I wanted to contemplate this lull in the middle of nothing that rose above the rest as the only secret I wanted to learn in life, to have control over it. Now, finally, there it is. I feel the wind ruffling my hair as if some great hand were caressing me, telling me that everything would be just fine.

Capitán Nemo, old man in the stern, seems to grasp it all newly through the whiteness of his eyes. He looks ahead, his hand steady, he's confident he knows the last route by heart, which will lead us to shore. What will he say when the boat finally touches land? I'm afraid, sure. But I'm also curious to know.

Octopus Ink

WAGNER'S ARMS WERE CROSSED behind the nape of his neck and his outstretched legs could almost touch the car's pedals. His seat was reclined and by the sound of his breathing, Ciro imagined he was asleep. He calculated another half-hour for the stakeout, thirty minutes was enough before people playing sports would vacate the seafront esplanade and the hookers would take their place, ensnaring tourists, trafficking in small quantities of drugs. They'd be here sooner or later, Ciro said to himself. Misconduct never arrives on time, but you can always count on it showing up. A few yards away, a mulatto woman with tangled peroxide curls jiggled her tiny hot pants as she passed by, a recognizable sign that dusk was looming over Río. Cyclists were on the return trip. Men in sweat suits. Preachers. Nothing out of the ordinary, he thought. Yet he felt somewhat downcast as he watched the woman walk into the distance, towards Calçadão de Matinhos, as if something were being lost with her. He dragged on his cigarette until his lips rubbed the edge of the filter. He exhaled. Tuesdays weren't meant for work-ing. They were for being in church praying.

Whenever Ciro wasn't smoking, he liked to roll a metal sphere around in his big black hand. He'd pause for a minute, and then rotate it around again. It had a soothing effect, he said.

"When you gonna quit playing with your damn balls?" Wagner said without opening his eyes.

"Ain't my balls," Ciro quipped. "They're my house keys. I have a gift from the Babalaô in my pocket, with my house keys and a chunk of . . ." he stopped. "Jobs like this stress me out."

"Just knock it off. You're stressing me out, too."

Vagrants. A few rushed pedestrians.

"The goddamn radio doesn't work . . ."

Wagner was the exact opposite of what one expected of a good paulista: he followed local soccer with devo-tion, he was a compulsive gambler, he was fun loving, and the most easy-going person he'd ever met on block. The fact that they'd taken him out of the favelas to work as a "tenderizer" in the southern district sent a clear mes-sage about last year's performance. Yet for some reason, he remained in Pinheiro's good graces, since even though he'd been relegated to minor jobs—petty theft, roughing people up, sheltering or disappearing snitches or people late on their payments—there weren't many bums who'd dare contradict him for fear of getting into a scrap with him, and it was a sound precaution to take, so long as his good luck with the boss lasted.

"You bet on Corinthians again?" Ciro asked.

It was an empty question, really, meant to keep Wagner from falling asleep.

"Two hundred bucks," he said coolly.

Enough not to sleep, enough not to stay awake. The goddamn limbo, the worst place a bet can take you.

Ciro nodded, staring out at the street.

Wasn't that what he always said? "This is going to ruin me, negro. I need limits." But he always went back: addicts inevitably slide back into their vices. Return to the scene of the crime, like murderers.

Out in the distance, the lights along the promenade looked like locusts, their intrusive eyes peeping above the palm trees. The sea was shivering a few hundred yards away, swells of soft, soundless waves. A couple strolled by nonchalantly: she swished her handsome mare's thighs as she walked, and he gently nudged her forward by the arm, as if the show of such a powerful woman made him suffer. It was hard to tell if they were lovers or just a prostitute and her john. He watched them walk, straight-backed, through the side view mirror until the reflection of his pockmarked face slid in front of the image, like a fly, which didn't seem as awful as he had remembered. If not for her, after all, he would never have met Melba and fallen in love. Melba would never have gone to bed with him in the first party in São João. And without that fine evening, in the gas station, he would never have brought her to live with him in São Clemente. He would never have gotten baptized. They wouldn't be expecting a child.

He brushed his cheek.

"You believe in luck, Wagner?"

Beside him, the seat squeaked like an old joint.

"Chance, you mean?"

"Luck, the kind some people have," Ciro said, shaking his head. "I mean what is it that makes a person be one way or another." He felt as though the right words weren't arriving on time. "I mean if you think a person might be so inclined that things come out favorably, or if a person does things that are either right or wrong because things could never be otherwise," he thought. "A world where there are no alternatives, not for anyone. Know what I mean?"

Wagner closed his eyes again.

"I don't claim to be some kind of philosopher, negro, but I can tell you one thing about luck. All *I* know is that over time luck doesn't loan anything out or give anything for free. It only collects." He clicked his tongue, as if something bothered him. "One way or another, any luck we have is because we've taken it away from somebody else."

He opened his eyes, as if hoping to see something.

"Make any sense to you, negro?"

"Yeah," Ciro said. "It makes sense."

Thirty years later, the only thing that remains of Praia Mansa is a thin echo of itself, a ridiculous leftover from the banquet that had devoured its own self. Not much left of the place where people used to gather on the warm sand to play soccer, even after the shore lost a good chunk to the constant tugging of the tide. The promenade had been flush with street stands and roving fairs and a deep-rooted festive vigor that now languished. It had inspired soft, sensuous, afflicted songs, poems dripping with melancholy, lovers declaring eternal devotion along the freshly polished cobblestone and swirling tiles that imitated in black and white, the movements of the sea. And now the hypnotic enchantment of this place, this imitation of the real, was spent, faded by mugginess and the passing years. Nobody seemed to miss its poetic esprit anymore, except a few old people who remembered seeing it on television or some mayor who remarked on how much it had given to the community that had reaped its benefits for forty years and grown as a result. Of course even now, in complete decadence, the prostitutes and grifters still do benefit, at the expense of clueless tourists and disenfranchised adolescents still roaming like specters where half a century ago the sea had swallowed a good piece of Atlantic Avenue.

You can still see its salty teeth marks along the embankment, above which scenic lookouts have arisen, besieged by clusters of stubborn weeds that are perfect for hiding assault and battery and guiltless homicides.

Truthfully now they were the only two people who could recall the apogee of this bend in the South Zone, playing dominoes in an old cubbyhole on Morro da Babilônia. Though his childhood memories spilled through him like a hot stream, his heart and mind preferred to remain silent, as if by their stillness they could occupy some other place, keep themselves safe from any softness. But there was something he couldn't avoid. And so Ciro waited, as he had sworn he would, for the first double tile to show its perfect symmetry of pips, to finally tell Cuaresma what he had come to say, before he came to look for him.

It took all of forty-seven minutes and three games for the moment to finally arrive.

"So it was true that they were out for me," Cuaresma said, self-possessed.

"That's what I heard."

The double sixes stood tall at the center of the table.

"Did they say why?"

Wagner says that Pinheiro dreamt about you twice this week. He saw a flower growing in the middle of a dark alley, cut it in half by a blade. Says he's been on edge lately, thinking about Mamboretá. He went to the Babalaô twice, and the Babalaô prayed and communed with the Orixás and found that the spirit of Yemanjá is calling for atonement because the war sullied his festival day. Anyway, the *viejo* thinks it's a good idea to wipe out anyone who survived *El Tatuado*. Babalaô didn't say as much, but he interpreted it to mean that someone in his crew is out for revenge against him.

He dried his forehead off with little taps of his handkerchief.

"You probably know by now, it started a few days ago," he said, and seconds later settled a few tiles on the table. "Belego showed up dead in Vidigal, shot in the head, and a few negros have disappeared inland with the excuse of picking up merchandise. Apparently he's still having dreams, and now you're the one he's most worried about."

Cuaresma shook his head blearily.

"You want my opinion, Ciro?" In no time, his long hand swallowed up one of the tiles. "It's been a long time since I heard something that idiotic. You think I never wanted it? For Christ's sake I'd do it with gusto. Lots of people would. But the way things are right now, I don't got money to buy a *faca*, let alone waste my time dreaming about it. Even if I had one, they'd never let me close enough to gut the son of a bitch. I'm at peace here, I work same as I did with Mamboretá. Nothing extra. Only a dumbass would think anybody could kill the old man with a *faca*, knowing he's got thirty dudes trailing every time he goes out."

"But that's the way it is," Ciro said, unsmiling. "I have to tell you there's already a date on your head."

"When?"

"The twenty-third." He thought again, "Or the twenty-fourth."

"Didn't give me much time now did they." His mouth stretched wide like a sash.

"So you agree, best you can do is make yourself scarce for a time, brother."

"Minas Gerais?"

"Any place you want, long as it ain't the coast."

"Guess I got no choice."

"Nope, no choice." Ciro was getting prickly, he couldn't help sweating like a pig. "You know it's my skin every time I give you the whistle, coming all the way out here, outside my zone. I mean, from now on I'll have to do it I run across you somewhere. Won't leave me no option. Melba's firstborn is coming in five months. A boy, Cuaresma. Can you imagine? No way she'd survive outside of Rio. Let alone, me, I don't go anywhere alone, even when I'm out cruising at night." He looked into his eyes, begging. "You know how it goes."

"Don't suppose I'll do anything stupid," Cuaresma said.

"Hell, you know I'd hate it if you did, brother."

"Yeah, I know. Me too."

They drank up their beers wordlessly till the bottle was dry and played until they lost count of the tiles.

"A boy then," Cuaresma said.

"Yeah: Brandão, like his grandfather. Sailor's name."

"With a name like that he'll always have somewhere to go. Could amount to something."

"Like you."

Cuaresma didn't seem all that convinced.

"Minas Gerais must be an eyeful this time of year."

"You bet. Anywhere outside Río will be more of an eyeful the rest of the year."

Watching the sun come up outside of the club full of bimbos and powerful creeps gave him callous-grade skin impervious to any other feelings. He watched the young girls dangling from tourists' arms, the young boys with painted lips, the elderly women stripped bare by drug addicts, apathetic, no sting of outrage. People were a strange kind of commotion to him, baffling. Ciro covered his ears, moved on. Same time every Tuesday he prayed beside the Babalaô with that fitting dream, thinking often in singular, every once in a while about Melba or his coming son, Brandão. The vagrants didn't matter to him now, the couples looking for dark thrills, the petty dealers who lost money, once their merchandise was bought they'd all crawl back into the hills with even less hope than before. Seeing Cuaresma five weeks ago made him think the vicious circle had finally closed. That he would get involved in something outside of his own life. He was mistaken, of course: domesticated dogs can never be chained too tightly to their conduct, their loyal temperament, their love of habit. He must have known that better than anyone.

The first prostitute arranged her tits in her white linen dress, and Ciro recalled how Wagner's high-pitched voice penetrated his dreams; it roused him again from that supple, placid torpor that Melba's food had brought on, and the ridiculous, tinny creaking of the door, like a hound, until the sharp wind reached his bedroom, his bed, the ceiling, and the deep cracks from the humidity that took him a few minutes to identify as his own.

When he opened his eyes, Melba stood staring at him, leaning against the door.

"Who is it?" Ciro mumbled.

"Wagner," Melba said.

She kept her mouth shut out of a controlled resolve. While he made out his wife's figure, split down the middle, the half moon of her belly poking out of her robe, he asked again, lying back on the bed.

"What does he want?"

"For you to come out," he said.

Ciro sat up in bed.

He rubbed his eyes.

"Yeah, Cuaresma, negro." The car growled impatiently at the door leading out to the street. "Remember how he got away last time?" Wagner leaned against the window, making room for the seat to come forward. "But I've been looking into it on my own. Asking around. And

this morning the German found him in Praia Mansa."
He lay back again. His back was aching. He didn't close
his eyelids again. Now he too looked over Atlantic Avenue, staring out at the pier. "All we have to do is make
sure the tip is good. You'd be able to identify him better
than me from up here. The viejo says he has the best eyes
in Río. 'By night he's like a black cat,' he said. 'His wrist
never shakes.'"

He got out of bed.

"Cuaresma?" Ciro asked in disbelief. "Are you sure
that's what he said, Melba?"

Ciro was skeptical now. But Melba was there with him:
he held her limp hand, fingers like boneless sponges, and
could tell she wasn't lying. He saw the way she nodded
her head slowly up and down.

"Cuaresma," the German said again, nodding. "The
same dude you were looking for. He came back today, I
saw him walking towards Babilônia. Alone."

"So he'll have to walk by here again," Wagner said,
exhaling a mouthful of smoke, "Sooner or later, the son
of a bitch will have to walk right in front of us."

Ciro squeezed the ball.

"We'll just wait, that's all."

That, and a couple of freshly loaded revolvers were all
that was on Wagner's mind. The rest, as always, was left
to improvisation.

Through the windshield, a black man threw stones at
the sand.

Three guys with pretty-boy faces hopped into a Land

Rover and disappeared. The third prostitute out adjusted her tits under an elastic tube dress. And in the night he could see her imitating the violet color of the sea. Vagrants. Drug addicts. A large man limping towards Mathinhos.

Ciro thought about the fake blonde again, but his sense of loss didn't return.

There he was.

Wagner poked his arm.

"Hey, negro," Melba said. "Eh, wake up, negro."

Cuaresma still thrashed around in Praia Mansa's wild scrub, he couldn't breathe, and pressed the top of his stomach as if something inside of him had broken. He was like a squirming fish suffocating outside of the water. Ciro laughed in front of him. He was holding the ball under his armpit.

"You going to roll around all day like a little baby, negrote?"

Cuaresma was coarse and clumsy, that's why Ciro always encouraged him to fight the bigger guys.

He stretched out his hand; but this time he didn't get up.

"You ok?" he said.

"You going to get up or do I have to kick your head in you wuss, you shithead?" Wagner walked back to where Ciro was. "How about we break his legs and then shoot him in the balls? Or kick him until he vomits his teeth out?"

Cuaresma looked at him the same way. The same washed out, yellow eyes. Though blood combed across his face, his moon-shaped features and shaved head were the same. Time had hardly changed a thing. Still the same stubborn negro who could never step away from a fight. Was he worth the risk he took? He could tell Wagner was waiting. He knew that a single word was enough to force a situation that never came; maybe to alter the order of that unmoving libretto they had imposed on each other long before seeing their faces through the glass. But even when he recognized him, when Wagner's husky frame blocked off any opportunity for escape, Cuaresma didn't say anything that could incriminate him, not even an appeal for mercy. Looking down from above, Ciro knew exactly what he had to do.

Pointing at the head has always been the easiest.

Which is what he did: he pulled the trigger.

"What the fuck did you do?"

"Didn't you see him?" The heat of the revolver clung to his hand. "I killed the asshole. Isn't that what Pinheiro wanted?"

"Yeah . . . fuck . . . but we were supposed to beat the shit out of him first. Didn't I say that in the car?"

Ciro looked at his wristwatch: it was nine thirty-seven at night.

"If we hurry, you can catch the second half of the game. I'm going to church to pray." His eyes surveyed the ground, the black stain was trickling closer to him, trying to touch his feet. "Both in peace, with our respective consciences."

"Negro, negro," Wagner said.

He walked back and dropkicked Cuaresma's head until he opened his skull. He did the same with his ribs and arms. He punted a while until Ciro finally stopped him.

"Now then, we're out of here," Wagner said, agitated. "Empty your load into him."

Ciro shot until his chamber clicked harmless as a lighter.

"Much better."

"Pinheiro will be happy now," Ciro said.

"Yup, let's get out of here."

They walked leisurely, crunching along the pebble-strewn ground. When they finally reached the yellow VW bug, even Wagner seemed to be in a good mood.

"Hey, the asshole stained my shoe."

The soft, yellow sodium lights along Atlantic Avenue seemed stitched to the shoreline by an unsteady pulse, all the way to Leme beach. A few girls walked along the shore arm in arm, like friends in a busy mall. Every once in a while one girl's hand slid with calculated gravity to skinny legs of the other's, or subtly stuck together, their behinds like a couple of buds ready to burst in their tiny bikinis. Playing with his metallic ball, Ciro felt immune to it all. The callus was now more like a stone. Though it was a stone with a pulse.

The car took off.

"Drop me off in São Clemente, okay?" Ciro asked, looking down the street, in the opposite direction they usually went.

But Wagner didn't answer.

The soaring buildings that passed as they drove in the metropolis seemed to him like tall, twiggy women draped in jewels, elusive and indifferent.

They glowed; the men only grew darker.

"Look at it this way," Wagner said, lighting a cigarette for him. "The Babalaô isn't going to feel bad cause you missed church today. Don't be stupid, Ciro. Me, I'd be grateful to Pinheiro if I was you, he gave you a stable job, good enough to think of a future, a nice place to bring up your boy. Not stupid, right? He always wanted you to take good care of his daughter. All he wants in return is for you to be grateful."

He drove to the outskirts of Tijuca in silence, near the woodlands and the darkened roads.

"Come on, let me buy you a beer while we watch the game."

Ciro looked at the dashboard's phosphorescence, keeping to sixty kilometers an hour. "Come on, it'll do you good. A couple of beers before church and prayer, eh?" He pressed the Beetle's accelerator. "A hundred and twenty *reales* on Corinthians. Can you imagine it negro? What we could do with all that dough?"

He laughed as he mulled over it, tasting it even, but he controlled himself.

Spaced residences. Long brick walls. Lights nearly at ground level.

Nothing seemed to end that night.

"Do you believe that Pinheiro dreamt of him, like he says?" Ciro wanted to fill his mind with other things, but he'd chewed on it for a while and needed to know now, while Wagner drove them to the place he knew they were headed. "I mean, let's be honest Wagner . . . just for once, say it . . . do you think any of this shit has anything to do with us?"

He knew his buddy was keeping a close eye on him, while watching the road.

It was part of the job.

"Want to know the truth, negro?" he turned around for two exact seconds, enough to show that his had suddenly gone vacant.

"Yeah, I'd like to know it."

"Fine," Wagner said, back on the path. "I'll tell you. His dreams were no more than octopus ink. Know what I mean?"

Ciro shook his head.

"Dreams only tell us what we don't want to hear. They dress up in masquerade to reach us. They scrape along, they trap us when we're at our most vulnerable and dump everything they're hiding on top of us." Now his voice sounded professional, neutral. "Like an octopus. They distract us with their black ink and then sneak away. They swim off, but leave us sullied with all the shit they have inside." He smiled. "Octopus ink. Sounds pretty good, huh?"

But Ciro didn't fully understand.

"Bah, negro, you'll figure it out when we get there."

"So it was only to keep us amused, huh?" he insisted anyway.

"Look at it like this," Wagner said. "If Pinheiro dreams, it ain't exactly about the dead.

Through the windows, Pinheiro's house and the cars parked around the dark entry hall were like little stains barely visible for the ghosts who guided them along. A short while later they took on concrete shapes, as Wagner had promised they would. Ciro thought again of Melba's profile. And squeezed hard at the metal ball in his pocket.

"He mostly dreams about the living," Wagner repeated, with a half-smirk that seemed menacing.

Somehow, Ciro was beginning to put things together.

"And he dreams about people who don't know they're alive yet," he said, seeing the people who were waiting outside.

"You're mistaken, Pinheiro thinks about them a lot, even when he's awake. People who don't realize it, and the ones who aren't entirely alive yet."

He glimpsed a silhouette beside the glass, just as the Beetle's engine cut.

"Better leave the keys in the ignition," Wagner said, opening his door. "Don't want them to think you're packing."

"Don't matter, Wagner. We both know mine could only make it here like a butcher without teeth."

Even still, feeling the fresh air slapping his face, Ciro left the keys and his gun on the dashboard.

"You think he'll take good care of him?" he asked.

They'd almost made the door when he said it.

"Yeah," Wagner said, annoyed. "Look at me."

He smiled.

"Your son's going to be a lucky man."

Turn Out the Next Light

For Hilda Codina

Let's just say, yes, the bus stops and an old man appears. A few heads look up, glimpse at him, then go back to hiding under the woven fabric. The people riding the regional bus snooze with the same coarse apathy of folks on their way to working in the fields. That's how they travel, twenty some miles down a barren spine of road, tucked under heavy blankets that keep them still and prolong the distractions of the trip till the city's huge concrete jaws swallow them whole. Usually at some point along the route, an illusory milepost brings them to a halt by a woman laden with bundles. The travelers watch anxiously as she boards, in case she's carrying pieces of jerky or corn bread in her pouches. If so, a mild commotion ensues as the commuters rouse themselves: people eat quickly, and just as quickly fall back asleep. But let's just say that this morning it's not her, but an old man who boards; the heads peeking out of the blankets watch him shuffle down the crowded aisle, but forget about him. While the others bundle themselves back under their blankets and the air's milky brume clings to the windows, veiling the first reed beds outside whose supple, luminous strands add new greenery to the semi-arid backlands, the old man shuffles along, making his way, and before long takes a seat. He clears his throat. He seizes his bag between his legs and waits for the wisdom of habit to acclimate his body, and his chin slowly drops towards his chest as he readies to take a snooze. But let's say that I decide not to let him have his catnap. Oh, just look at the cagey, exception-taking expression on his face now.

"Antônio Honorato da Silva," I say to him. "Forty-seven years ago, you were in the Alagoas detachment that prevailed in the Porta da Folha offensive, during the wee hours of July 28, 1938. You, sir, have the same gaunt face and sun-bronzed skin as you had back then, though now you're no more than a stooped old man in glasses who thinks his glories past still give him reason for arrogant self-importance. I'm pretty sure the old Honorato, the one I knew way back when, is an open wound for me alone now; maybe his name is no more than a branding iron, and thinking about it, it's the only reason we'd meet forty seven years later on this bus on its return trip. It was Antônio Honorato, you—or at least his eyes in happy confusion—who shot the rifle that left Virgulino Ferreira, Lampião, dead in a grove in Sergipe, on Angico Ranch, while he and María Bonita were fast asleep. I have a clipping folded into eight equal parts of the newspaper story that came out three days afterwards, and there's a black and white photograph of you. Want to see it? Look, there's Private Antônio Honorato smiling and holding his rifle, the dry shells in palm of his hand, and there's my dead brother's head, in a town square in Bahía."

JORNAL DO COMMERCIO—JUNE 12, 1938

Paraíba—In their commentaries on the recent summit between the Pernambucan police force and Lampião's band, newspapers underscore our current State government's new and determined approach towards finding a solution to the troubling problem of banditry sweeping long stretches of the Sertão region. In today's edition of *A União* we acknowledge the measures of our brave law enforcement agencies to reinforce the border region given the possible emergencies that could arise in the coming days. As is public knowledge, the latest deadly confrontation between the police and the *Cangaceiro* bandits led by the notorious brigand Virgulino Ferreira, a.k.a. Lampião, took place in the municipality of Lagoa do Crauá, Sergipe, which terminated when said leader suffered a fatal bullet to the hip by Bahian troops under the command of José Osorio de Farias, Zé Rufino. As could later be verified, Lampião's gang of outlaws numbered 67 men, the largest operating in the northeastern territory to date. Nine bandits and three policemen were reported dead in combat. Arms and weapons seized include a 1908 Mauser rifle and three Colt .38 revolvers, or Colt Cavalinhos as said firearms are otherwise identified. The Authority's ongoing investigation provides clear information pointing to the gravity of the conflict. It is expected that full respect and compliance be shown these measures in the coming days, designed to protect the security of the citizenry.

"You headed for Serra Talhada then?" the old man asks me after a while, scratching his head.

"Yaw, Serra Talhada," I nod. "Thirty-five years later."

"Little late to be chasing memories there," Honorato adds, "but it's good to return to your birthplace, a way of closing things that might not of turned out too well. I imagine things didn't turn out so good if you're heading back that way now, eh? See, back in the day, Serra Talhada used to be called Villa Bella, might be called something different now, but nothing's changed; barren and inhospitable as always, and I bet the folks, if there are any left, only stay there to die. What'll it be like? If it's people you're looking for, won't be the same, surely. Most everybody took off to try his or her luck in other towns. The big southern states. Same as anywhere else now, only commerce left is for the landless, and lately they're the ones who own the land that belonged to landowners and colonels before, even though they make people call them 'the landless.' Damn! No need for machetes or rifles no more; just gather a horde and that's enough for the kind of people left in Pernambuco. Turned Serra Talhada into a place of their own, nothing like it used to be. Like every other where too; every borough, city, town, don't matter, done the same thing. Don't you see? There are decent places in Pernambuco, like all over, surely, but not the place you're coming. You'll see. And when you get there, you'll think on what I said right here, on this road right here, that what old Honorato da Silva said wasn't wrong."

"You don't live in the region anymore?" I ask him.

"No, I don't live there anymore . . ." the old man says. "Been a long time since then."

"And now?"

But the old man didn't seem interested in answering me. Antônio Honorato gripped his newspaper as if he were recalling something too personal, and I took advantage of his truce to breathe in the sudden nostalgia, contemplate the sea of bowing reeds in front of my eyes, miles and miles of them gently combed by the wind. Observing the meager, weather-beaten folk who inhabit these semi-arid backlands, it's hard to imagine so much violence out there still. But their belligerence isn't born of selfishness; it's part of their nature, what moves them forward. The warm womb alight inside, like an instinct that as much dwells in them as in the primordial places of this rough-hewn land, people forced to battle their milieu over every inch of its wrathful geography, forging their character with what is the most essential. Fury that bleeds into the sky at dusk. Drought. Deathly poison. Beside me, the old man studies the same landscape I'm interpreting, in my own way; then he looks at me and I at him finally, and I know he's come back to the world with me.

"I have a shack about forty kilometers northeast of here, along the Alagoas border. There's a small farmstead there that the peasants haven't seized yet. It's all I have, ain't much now, but it's mine. I know they're coming though." He surveys the panoramic view, the vast reed fields waiting to be cultivated as soon as winter's over. "They sure are coming. And when they do, I'll be waiting."

* * *

Seventy some miles down, the man tightens his horse's bridle and lets it stay there: same robust, resolute tension he uses to break in the stubborn mules; same aloof, solitary, distracted expression. The well-spoken beast quiets down. Neighs some, but then the muscles ease up fine. Pedro Cândido, the *Coitero*, said it's over there, go on inside now, and there among the bales of hay he slept, ate, and drank, though the steed watered from the trough just half way through the journey, good way to sidestep any run-ins with others. The *volantes* had been circling his hideout. Then they rode hard, it seems. He, too, in his own way. So much so that finally he's got the São Domingos riverbank in front of him, and in front of that, the family shack he hadn't been to for such a long time.

"Whoa!" he sounds, pulling on the bridle, patting the animal's neck: its strong hide, its chestnut mane a noble sight; pure Pernambucan Sorrel. He, too, examines the savannah, the faded *caatinga* scrub like strands of hair; the shed just down yonder, the cabin he left for the last time five years ago, carried that same familiar confusion he feels each time he looks in the mirror's silver surface and sees the youthful expression that no longer seems the right attire for him. So here we are now. Done that trail better than anyone—he tells himself, looking ahead—we've come back together. He pats the horse's haunches: yeah, you know it, too, don't you, boy. He calculates some nine leagues of barren land and there's the sheer hunchback mountain where strange red-hued clouds gather around its summit. Caruaru is behind that: a thirteen hour even trot, maybe twenty—at a brisk pace—to Porta de Folha should a patrol show up. He jerks the horse's muzzle; don't matter the *Volantes* are looking for him; the bronco kicks up dirt with the clip-clop of her hooves. A flock of finches takes flight in the opposite direction and the golden shape they outline in the sky projects a languid shadow, not enough to appease the heat of the ride. He shields his eyes with his open hand beneath his hat and as the woman who's been waiting for him approaches, he thinks how a man can leave many different places, but only one, truly, ever welcomes him back.

"Good day, brother," the girl says.

"An embrace, little one."

Analia is now a high-spirited fourteen-year-old, petite and narrow-hipped, she turns halfway around to accommodate his pace, hurrying to collect the Sorrel and straighten its path towards watering trough, tugging at its bridle with an adult woman's skill. The man follows a few paces behind, waves of emotion stirring inside, snaking along the soil burnished by other men's horseshoes. These first signs of weakness remind him that he's now walking towards the only place he belongs. That belongs to him. But they've been here too, he knows, and he'd better move fast.

"You've been on the road for five days," Anália says when they get to the shade.

"Three, from Sergipe."

"Then three, same difference. How long you here for now, can I know?"

He shrugs his shoulders. "Don't know. You?"

She shrugs.

They laugh.

Then the laughter wears out and all that's left is the man's questions.

"Mother?" he says, finally.

Anália points towards the house.

"Inside. You know where."

There were seven of them, if I'm not mistaken. Virgulino was the third. That's certain. He fancied playing the eight button accordion, liked to work leather, broke mules in and all kinds of mountable beasts, rode anything with haunches, till one day he mounted a mare and never got off, never even said goodbye. They'd already killed his daddy and he got all obsessed with the Colonels. I'll bring justice to Pernambuco, he used to claim, though we all said bah, just a boy's swagger. But he came through in a way, don't you see? He went after those landowners, those Colonels.

Sinhô Pereira up and took him one day: that old bandit was notorious back then, and we didn't hear from Virgulino till he came back a commander, showed up one day by way of Jauzeiro, now a Captain of a bunch of kids who came with him, wearing leather hats upturned, galloping around and shooting off their rifles. Virgulino was now Lampião, he said. The saintly hand of Father Cícero blessed it. And that's how it was; from then on it was epic. He brought extravagant things to share around. Food. Chachaça. And people helped him; stealing things from the Colonels was legitimate. Zé Rufino was after him by then, no small thing. He came-and-went . . . Worked seven states that way, see? From Ceará to Bahía, the whole Northeast belonged to Lampião and his eighty kids who followed him wherever he went, all equals, all armed to the teeth, made you feel humble to see them. Didn't forget no one. People were good to him, but then the *Volantes* came and that was something different. So tell me where'd he go? So what'd he say? On the lookout for anything. But no ahhh, no nothing. Folks in Serra Talhada loved him. See? Gave me a safe-conduct: *Recebendo carta com a minha firma, não sendo este cartãozinho, é falsa. Não é minha assinatura.* See that? Then on, whenever I rode around the Caatinga with the cowboys, all I had to do was show my letter and there was peace. The real thing, respect.

"I dreamed you were coming . . ."

"Mamãe," the man says, bending over the bed.

His lips kiss her salty skin, already scarce as the sunrise. There, by her side now, the irreversible furrows of premature old-age push him gently to the side for the first time, and he, distraught, moves away from the scent of his memories of days gone by, and gazes at his mother sideways.

"Sit down," she says.

"I've been in the saddle for three days," he moves aside brusquely to stop staring at her, "riding the dry earth through the night. Let me just stand here and look at you like this, from on high."

"Never were one to come down from there," his mother sighed. "Rightly so, you were born to be up there, I knew since you was a boy. That's what brings you here now, to see your mother again; no matter what they said: the *macacos* are after him night and day, nobody can knows where he is, no. How can you hope to see him again, you being a woman, and old at that? But they're always wrong . . . a mother always makes a way to see her children."

"Or the children let themselves be found sometimes."

"Speak too soon." She pokes at the air with her finger. "I dreamt that you were coming . . . dreaming is a way of searching. You couldn't carry on without saying goodbye to this old woman."

"You shouldn't age so quickly, Mãe."

"One doesn't decide such things," she says, lowering her head. "But listen, my boy, better we don't talk about me. I know you don't have long."

"I've seen the burnished earth . . ." the man hastens, "Zé Rufino and his *Volantes* must have come through earlier."

"They're always here. They come often, for whatever reason. You must have seen them, the posters they hand out now, rewards hung around the streets, fifty gold coins . . ." the old woman crosses a charitable glance, as if she weren't speaking of her own son, "and I tell your sister that any day now those *macacos* are going to have a good shot at you."

"That's foolish, Mamãe. If I had as much money as they say, I wouldn't be thieving Colonels."

"I know you don't do it for the money."

"It's always for the money, Mamãe. You know that."

They remain silent for a while, but the old woman watches him, moving his head with an abrasive affection that cuts through her pupils.

"Is it true he's already dead?"

"Don't know," the man answers. "I give it my best, you know. I shoot every soldier I see."

* * *

Let's say that, yes, the old man settles in beside me. Let's say I call him "Antônio Honorato da Silva," thinking aloud, really. So he looks at me, annoyed; he stares at me. Finally his suspicion subsides (maybe because he sees I'm a woman) and doesn't hesitate to answer me directly: yes, that's my name: Antonio Honorato da Silva. I talk to him about Porta de Folha, forty-seven years ago, and that I have several newspaper clippings, one of them with his photo, folded into eight equal parts. I don't say anything about my dead brother; only that I know the story. A stiff smile twists upward at the side of his lips then, and he says he's proud of having done his job, though the credit, as always, was given to the higher-ups; João Bezerra, in my case. But they continued hunting the rest of them, Gato and Corsico; and it was José Rufino who got there first, and gained fame at his expense. Not many remember Bezerra now, which is only fair.

"What's that medal around your neck?" I ask.

"Nice, isn't it?" his eyes slitting: "'Private da Silva: for bravery.' If only I had a little courage now . . . don't mean to be sentimental; everyone knows memories don't buy the groceries, unless you sell them."

I ask him if the medal was for killing Limpião.

He says yes.

"None other than Virgulino Ferreira himself," he said after a while, without pride. It was by virtue of shooting quickly. Hard not to kill a man that way, after Pedro Cândido told us where he was sleeping with the rest of the kids that night. All the same, we brought a few *costureiras* with us, to be sure we killed him good and dead. Machine guns, see? He'd gotten away too many times, and every man, no matter how much of an enchanter, has a limit.

Up ahead someone gets off the bus and the fan of dawn blows through the open door in gusts: it takes a few minutes for them to retrieve the bags from the roof, we hear a dry thud; then a strangely detached voice saying it was alright, move on, and a little while later I see a sign pass by, a few huts, and finally the range of arid land that's accompanied us the past four hours.

"Are you a journalist?" he asks abruptly.

"I'm a teacher," I say.

"Sorry to hear that . . . I mean that you're not a journalist. Twenty years ago, they interviewed me for *O'Globo*, in *Região*, and even a Salvadoran radio station. Not long ago I was told that they're filming people . . . but they only talked to Bezerra and Zé Rufino. And a few old civilians, there was one, especially, who talked about what a hero

Limpião was for his people. I saw him on television seven years ago, and they talked pure foolishness. It was the anniversary. See? Once, on my way back from Bahía with the unit, I came across Otacío Macedo, the journalist, and he promised a big cover story, full color. But I never saw him again."

For a moment he gets lost again in that promise; then he looks at the seat left vacant by the absent passenger, and a little while later comes back with a new spark in his eyes.

"If I may say as much, an old man is always looking for someone to acknowledge him. Even if a stranger, like yourself."

"Even if it's because you killed a man?"

He thinks.

"Even for that: an old man is nothing more than a silly man who doesn't want to die."

Regardless, I find it impossible to acknowledge my brother's murderer in that man. I'm over fifty years old now, and it's on account of men like him that I realize there's always room for wonder. I wouldn't say the same thing of this land, filled with blood and protest, but it is what it is. A person lives in a constant state of surprise. Even when it seems as though nothing can possibly surprise you anymore. Meanwhile, the old man takes some nuts from his pocket. Still clutching the stiff cloth bag between his legs, he opens the nuts with his hard, colorless, nails. He brings them mechanically to his mouth and chews slowly; when he's finished, he still remembers what I said when I introduced myself.

"So you're returning to Serra Talhada," he scratches his head.

"Yes, Serra Talhada," I nod. "After thirty-five years away."

There are miles and miles of Caatinga in the Northeast: arid earth, wavy cacti, droopy seedlings, fickle needles remembering a time before memory when only reptiles walked the land. But look, ages ago men and women conquered this hostile territory. Showed up one day and never left. Settled. And now, along this vast coastal territory, fields of reeds flourish, their green, sharp-edged leaves like tresses trembling in the breeze, never tire of growing. The day awakens with a vegetable murmur, colors dissolve orange-yellow-blue. Till dawn breaks.

Then, throughout that savage territory, small camps, groups of families rise with the first sounds, they gather and peer into the distance to detect the regional bus, which rattles and bangs through the ribbons of reeds, squashed under a mountain of rucksacks and belongings loaded on its roof. The rucksacks are sturdy and well tied so that nothing falls out, though some of strings dangle like ivy vines over the window, and somebody's field-worn, weather-beaten face looks out over the landscape being left behind. Goodbye land, goodbye!

If you could follow us now, you would see an old man

inside, who rushes down the aisle and makes it to the door without tripping, avoiding legs and packages uncovered by the freshly awakened ponchos. He's the one who bends to whisper something in the driver's ear and a moment later, the only passenger who gets off when the bus comes to a stop. The man hops off without looking back, without even waving. All he said was that he was sorry, and that such is life in the *Cangaço*, and now he's no more than an old man with nothing to live for except that death. I don't know what to say. Except to wish him luck with the "Landless," who I will be teaching at the school in Serra Talhada. He looks at me, I look at him, and that's it. The entire scene. No melodrama. So when I watch him get off, there's no need for him to say good-bye once the advancing bus has reduced him to nothing more than the last vacant seat around me. The bus growls again, with that sickly cough that keeps it moving forward, and I glance out the window at the street where the old man is far away now amid the dust and the multitude. Framed by streets and stones, the reed fields are now reduced to hundreds of bales strung together into huge mounds: and there walks old Honorato, lost among the shops. I watch him, through the glass, those few dirty seconds it takes him to move in the opposite direction, shrinking as we advance, slowly, little by little, until soon he disappears altogether.

I look down the aisle at the people who are now wide awake. I hear a few giggles, the cranky seats complaining, and the persistent sound of a throat being cleared, as if trying to untangle the spider's web that the mugginess has woven in one of these chests. Everyone's awake, like you, Anál...a, I say to myself. But it's all I think. Nothing else. I'm no longer clutching the knife that I swore I'd bury in him that afternoon when I first saw his photograph in the newspaper, together with Virgulino and María Bonita's heads. My brother's and his wife's heads. My whole family. Dead. But it's also true that I left the *faca* in a closet full of memories, who knows why, maybe so I wouldn't be carrying it today, when chance placed me face to face with the glaring light that dwells at the depths of my Northeastern blood. Let's just say that in the end, it could have risen at the wrong time.

JORNAL DO COMMERCIO—JULY 29, 1938
Paraíbo—The State of Sergipe announces that yesterday, in the wee hours on July 28, the police force of Alagoas, led by João Bezerra da Silva, gunned down eleven of the most sought after *Cangaceiros* in Angico grove, in the municipality of Porta de Folha, Sergipe. Among the dead is the Pernambucan leader Virgulino Ferreira, a.k.a. Lampião, who fell before Private Antônio Honorato da Silva's perfect shot. He perished beside his concubine, Maria Gomes de Oliveira, a.k.a. María Bonita. According to information provided by the Military Police, forty-nine heavily armed policemen launched the attack, which lasted fifteen minutes, and it's estimated that some

twenty-five bandits evaded capture, whose search and sei-
zure is underway by authorities on the southern bank of
the river São Francisco. Photo (from left to right) Quinta
Feira, Luiz Pedro, Mergulhao, María Bonita, Lampião,
Eléctrico, Caixa de Fósforo, Enedina, Cajarana, Dife-
rente and an unknown citizen. The heads of the deceased
Cangaceiros were exhibited in the zone, together with their
belongings and confiscated munitions. With this severe
and effective action, our State Government has struck a
blow to banditry and is well on the path of eradicating its
ruinous presence in the Sertão region.

Time to go, I whisper, and clutch the hat I'm holding in
my hand; but nobody answers me here, nobody moves.
Only moths fluttering about the oil lamp, they whirl like
flower petals in the wind: they move clumsily, geometri-
cally, bumping the sides of the screen with a quiet noise,
lightly electrical, hesitating. I perceive the labored balance that looks for light in the delicate flapping. It's the
potent vertigo they have to struggle against their entire
short lives, I tell myself. The oil lamp, its quiet glow, the
deep well that pulls in the levity of their flight, their up-
and-down, as if that hole of light, in the darkness, were
an abyss. I stare for a long time at the light buzzing inside
the little box, the struggling moths, and don't dare utter
a word.

She's struggling too, I tell myself: I watch her breathe,
and yet she wakes up. Mamãe . . . She opens her eyes,

and that calm, inner glow fixes on me, as if she had forgotten she could communicate using her timeworn, high-pitched voice, and it was her turtle eyes that searched for mine as the only means she had to communicate. It's late, I say: a good day is always too long for her son Virgulino. The *Volantes* will be coming soon, and they'll take me if I stay. She smiles finally, or maybe it's only the reflection of a flame flickering under the screen. We look at each other for a while. She licks her lips and nods.

I turn out the light, kiss her salty skin and leave for Angico. I ride the horse hard so as not to think about the women. In Anália, who waited by the door with my saddle ready. My mother, sleeping. And yet, I think, far from here, Virgulino Ferreira will ride that steed hard and soon he'll arrive in the grove where María Bonita awaits, with the rest of the kids, to follow my trail tonight. María Bonita is there, taking care of my accordion; it's the image that gives him strength to remain in the saddle, stiff reins belting the horse forward, across the plains where the reeds rustle in the wind, moving like strands of hair, only ninety miles left to reach the bank of the São Francisco. In truth Virgulino knows, as the others do, that he'll never return to his land. But that's the deep way that life shines. And it's the way it should be.

Those Who Wait

*"Vriel interpretatur ignis Dei, sicut legimus apparuisse
ignem in rubo. Legimus etiam ignem
missum desuper, et inplesse quod praeceptum est."*
San Isidoro, Etymologiae, *V, 15*

1.

IT WAS A SUN-DRENCHED DAY and so humid the whole
city seemed to stick to the skin with that light lift of dried
puddle leaves. The photographer, whose last name was
Balbín, had stood up—maybe on account of it being so
muggy—and I imagined the sweat stains along his back
that left a map of his posture in repose, as he walked from
me and toward the window, huffing and puffing. They
told us we had to wait. The room was large, and we had
a few sofas to rest on. That's why at first it didn't bother
me. I figured if each one of us kept entertained by staring at the fan as it wrestled with the weather, we might
just make the heat subside and accomplish some kind of
small victory over nature. But Balbín got the big idea of
asking me for a *pucho*, from the Quechuan *puchu* meaning

something leftover, as in surplus or residue, I recalled. I would have very happily said there's one in my pack of cigarettes if that had been the case. But the paper rolled fat with tobacco hadn't been touched by fire or by mouth, not by any other form of drag; it was no leftover, no butt, it was intact, and for however much I would have loved to comply, it was no *pucho*: it was just a measly cigarette. I glanced at the painting of a couple that hung on the wall, and told him I didn't have one. That he could imagine being in someone else's company had hurt my feelings, and I was making him pay for it. I guess I, too, was wallowing in the exactitude of my own selfishness, though strictly speaking I didn't lie. Protected by etymological correctness, I thought: everything born of the mind is a lie.

Lie or no lie, Balbín didn't like the answer.

I watched him fiddle with his camera and focus on the rest of the room, as if I didn't exist.

When I want to amuse myself, all I have to do is draw on my good memory, and words flutter to me like moths looking for light; then I preserve them with the collector's gentle decorum and observe them, tugging at their membranes, as if they were no longer alive. Like my father once said to me: if you know the origin of something, you know its destination. I suppose the same can be said for certain people. Monster (from *monstrare*) is a good example. Up to the seventeenth century deformed people birthed by human womb, were considered a manifestation of something. Not just tricks of nature, as Aristotle thought, but signs that could be read, interpreted, and propagated; sort of like the news in a daily paper. The bodies of monsters were like writing instruments telling of what had happened and what should happen. They were words in flesh, and words never lied, they just appeared and one had to learn how to read them; and that's all.

"I don't have one," I said again, so Balbín could hear me.

But I made the mistake of suddenly hankering for a smoke, and so I inadvertently patted my bag and Balbín must have noticed, because a little while later he asked me again and I said no again.

"It's not a butt," I said.

He answered, "And we who are so accustomed to stumps." Both of us, who understand the codes, ended up having a good laugh.

Atanasio alone had been able to walk through the length of beaded curtains, whose entrance rippled in a slight wave-like motion like a nervous, wakeful jellyfish and we, too, watched as his shadow was sucked into its tentacles, our friend's shadow, swallowed by that other darkness. The feeble light filtering through the window seemed to wrinkle the objects, aging them, and suddenly all of it made me feel stricken. I didn't like the hard shells of fabric covering the sofas. It made me think of the dead. And then there was this: the waiting room smelled like something dusty and about to crumble in our fingers.

And everything, in the precariousness of whatever was in transit between those fingers, looked forsaken to my eyes.

2.

I had worked at the newspaper until late in the afternoon the day before. And still I had traveled by plane, and then by van, and half an hour after arriving I was peacefully asleep in this town. That's not what was on my mind, though, when they told us to wait. On the contrary, I began thinking about words. And when I got bored with that, I started to remember.

I reminisced, for example, on the time when my grandmother used to knit me scarves, back when I was still a boy and could never have imagined I'd end up roaming near and far looking for monsters. I recalled those blank and peaceful hours sitting beside her and watching her nurture the fabric: the rhythm of her wrist strokes, the needles still waging a battle against wrinkles. Time that seemed trapped in that simulacrum of stitches that would fall like ripe fruit beside her house slippers once it reached the limit of willpower and could hold on no longer. I own up to the fact that I was never able to fully coil those endless tongues of wool around my neck. I was little then, and I could wrap their hoofed mammal warmth around me five or six times and then some. I liked to gussy up in front of a mirror and go outside swathed in her interminable knitted hug, a charm so that nothing could ever hurt me.

"Seems like a lot of prayer goes on around here," Balbín said.

I brushed my memories aside, as if I'd hung them on a hoof, and followed the direction of his finger. He said, "Nothing we haven't seen already."

Right there, above the entry door, hung a huge Popsicle stick cross that was varnished with such a high-gloss polish it reminded me of an ex-girlfriend's nails. Never trusted that one, and when I asked her to remove the polish, she took off with some fella who used hair gel. Plaster cast figures were scattered here and there, angels and saints, small religious depictions. A glow-in-the-dark rosary hung draped over the edge of a bookcase, and a painting of Jesus's Sacred Heart hung above the slit leading to the next room: it was nailed just above the curtain of beads that undulated with each incursion of the tenuous breeze.

Balbín, who found it all blasé, had already distanced himself from the scene; but I stayed put, my eyes fixed on the Baroque painting in front of me, the faint tarnish consuming the golden frame, its bas relief, the swollen contours of Jesus Christ, like the veins of an arm being forced to exert itself. That's when it happened, when that exertion called forth another memory. I thought about myself and felt alone; I had decided not to believe in anything a long time ago, and though I tried hard to pray, I couldn't anymore. Jesus Christ was the same as ever, and that was never going to change: an amber halo glowed from behind his long, chestnut locks, and he was baring his open palms, penetrated by the absence of a nail, revealing an open heart, choked in barbs and flames.

Balbín said something else, but I didn't hear him. I found that I was traveling towards other objects in the house. I focused my distraction on one of the paintings hanging on another wall, the only one free of the room's over-saturation of flea-bitten furniture and poorly stowed poverty, which greeted us on the way in and stuck to our pants like a burr ever since. I recognized the woman in the portrait, and smiled at how clear-sightedly she had earmarked the best spot in the house to place a souvenir of herself.

Earlier, she had opened the door and asked us to wait, and we'd obeyed her. But it wasn't until later that I put it together, when I recognized her beneath all the wrinkles and makeup. The painting belonged to her; it was a typical marriage portrait. The man was dressed in a black suit with rose-brushed cheeks, his jaw set sternly and his expression serene as he peered out at some point lost in the glare of light that I now occupied. I gathered that he was the groom; beside him, she wore a flower-print dress, and tried to hold her ample, peach-sized cheekbones still.

I arrived at the following conclusion: I'd have forgotten about these two people completely, if it hadn't been for the colors that were used to fill them in.

Maybe it's something I dreamed, but at a certain point I realized that the camera had stopped making noise and I opened my eyes.

"Come here," Balbín said.

A boy with snot-crusted nostrils was peeking through the beads.

"Come on over, sport," he insisted.

But the boy, impervious, looked straight through us. His belly was perfectly round and he was sucking on a finger for lack of a sweet. The beads hiding him looked like tiny chocolate balls dipped in colorful candy coating. I felt sorry for him and sensed tears welling inside of me. Then a teenage girl appeared, could've been his sister, and took his hand. His sandals slapped like an aggrieved applause that faded into someplace that was out of our sight.

I must have spent the following five minutes in a deep slumber, because when I awoke, or thought I awoke, Balbín was shaking my arm or my shoulder and I left the painting behind again, with its artificial colors that were distorting the couple's past. Like a zombie, I tried to gain command of my muscles as best I could, and grappled to follow after him, far from the sofa. Balbín advanced and I followed him, I could swear I was floundering. We crossed the dining room in the dark, the kitchen in the dark, a coop of clucking hens in the dark, and still the asphyxiating colors of that room continued to paint my retina with the color of poverty and the most pauperized faith (from the Latin *pauper*, -èris), which means barren, I recalled; the sterile and aching color of a condition that produces nothing, not even in resistance to sorrow.

I couldn't explain where we were until we reached the girl's bedroom, where everything, for the first time that afternoon, was infused with a new, luminous color. This too is true; such was the indolence and odor of that room where they made us wait. And if it hadn't been because my eyes and mind dried up right away, I might have been able to comprehend a little more clearly what would happen later. A little bit. But instead, all I saw was the woman with long braids, who now, with the wrinkles she didn't have in the portrait, said to us, "It's your turn to suckle, sir."

I had just crossed the threshold and couldn't quite say what it was that most disturbed me about that scene, whether it was the smell of her exposed maternity now drying up, or the modest way she picked her up daughter in her arms and arranged her braids while storing her exposed right breast as if it were a delicate trophy.

"The girl," Atanasio said. "We would like to see the girl, Señora."

"Yes, yes," the woman said.

It lasted five or seven minutes more or less. Finally someone closed a door, one of those high, solid wood doors that goes all the way to the ceiling; and the mother of the small prodigy we were there to meet and display to the world snapped to again, quit arranging her braids and the huge breast took its place and she sat down on the bed. The baby was swaddled in felt from head to toe like a tiny babushka.

"Adorable girl," Balbín said.

And the woman and a scrawny little girl both began peeling the creature. We took this trip to prove it wasn't just another one of many, and the tiresome setback irked me, like when someone stands in line for hours only to find that the event he was waiting for was already over. I was accustomed to the opposite happening. I mean, I'd been always hoped to find something that didn't surprise me; and always, no matter how common it was, I ended up staggered at how creative nature can be.

I was about to acknowledge that Balbín was right, when the woman took it upon herself to anticipate things: she pulled up the little robe that covered the girl and the crude dishcloth she was wrapped in slipped off, curling around an irregular hazelnut-hued comb of vertebras. I let her work alone, and soon enough the entire back was exposed: that's when she turned her over and showed us the full naked splendor.

"*Her back*," the woman said, as if trying to draw attention to it by naming what it wasn't.

We got it.

Silently, Bablín set his machinery in motion again.

"Your daughter is so cute," he said, after a while. "Can you hold her in your arms now?"

The mother nodded at his request; she took up one of

the arms that fell from the child's back, and showed it in a close-up that later became the front page before. She extended it like a braid and combed it with caresses, while the two other little arms, wrinkled like a pair of dried vegetables, dropped nearly to her waist. Atanasio began asking and the mother answering, with pained gestures, as if she were no longer talking about herself but some neighbor who had been visited by tragedy, maybe even death.

"Maybe you can explain to me how a girl can be born with four arms," the woman said. "Her father was my cousin, you see, must be his fault the way he boozed. Where's the jerk now?"

Atanasio, writing, aha, he was your cousin, aha, he boozed, aha, where is he now. The whole time, the constant sound: *click click click click*. The sound of photos being taken, until the sound stopped.

Which is when Balbín said, "All set."

"You see Señora, it was easy."

I had seen Atanasio fill his notebooks with the same sloppy, untamed blue handwriting, with which he now signed the contract where the mother agreed she wouldn't receive another thing from us. He looked at me after signing his name, satisfied, then closed the notebook and quickly stuffed it into his trouser pocket.

"See how easy?"

And then, looking at Balbín, she said she was hungry.

"Yeah," Balbín said, tiresomely.

He placed a couple of crumpled bills in the woman's

hand. And again the darkness, and the light of day.

Julito Mora was waiting for us outside, catching a snooze in the van. In our absence the town of bare bricks and dirt roads filled with a white glare that hurt our eyes. We left the town in an optimistic mood; we looked for a place to eat, and could hear doors closing to the bark of dogs, while our editor-in-chief, Atanasio Matienzo, once again prophesied what was going to happen in the world. It had become a custom: Atanasio would look at Balbién's photos and predict what would happen in the country, and we would approve his verdict, or better said, I would, as director of the newspaper. I looked at the desert and a few crumbling houses on the other side of the window and remembered how the desert (from the Latin, *desertus*) derives from the verb *deserere*, which means to forget and, at times, abandon.

I wanted to do both.

Shortly a parking space opened up after a while, the four of us then sat down in a market stand and ordered whatever they were serving. Atanasio perused his notes and said, "*Locust girl claims hunger and thirst in northern Peru.*"

For some reason, I recalled the colorless painting in that house; and the mother inside her layer of wrinkles, swaying back and forth as if she were nodding at everything going on around her, observing Atanasio scratch the whiskers below his cheeks, that young prophet's beard of his, and I had no doubt that things were going to be the way he pronounced. Balbín continued melancholically, caught in the never-ending search for the image; but Julito Mora, the driver, polished off his beer toasting to the drought and famine to come.

3.

Like I said: eight hours later there they were, the photo and the headline, on "Little Monkey" Aguilar's screen. I still remember it clearly, because it was only six months before Johnny Benavente, who'd been scripting police procedurals for fifteen years, wrote a magnificent chronicle on the strange case of encephalocele in the high Andean plateau that I praised personally and ordered that it be published. We knew about her origin, we could name her condition without sounding incompetent: we could name the causes, give statistics, describe the expected deformities, that sort of thing. But really, that story had been written about the Macusani girl, and how the protrusion of bone matter that lay docilely over the vertebra of her neck wasn't due to science but by and large to superstition.

By the time the story began circulating throughout the city, the parish priest had refused to baptize the girl twice; and due to a minor bit of popular indignation (at times originated by other people's misfortune), the paper was inundated with letters the entire week. Until then, we had nearly always given the prophecies an infallible form of resolution: the future was long and any evil, though imminent, was better kept at a distance. Benavente, who came from a different school, nevertheless added a new twist to our custom: seeing the girl's deformity, he decided to arrange his investigative puzzle as if what he had before him was a *corpus delicti*, asking whether the girl's physical excess wasn't perhaps the sign of lost faith in favor of secular reason, and the proof was in the elusive cerebellum's failed attempt to be born by escaping through a gap in the skull.

Atanasio agreed it was a risk, but eventually accepted *the allotment of Providence* and left it up to me. We weren't sorry. The body's overflow of cartilage and skin finally made sense two weeks later when a mudslide swept the Town Hall away one night in 1991. This time Balbín accompanied Benavente: the mayor was buried beneath that fateful quagmire, along with the municipality's top brass, and a group of ill-starred Aymaras who were resisting the government, about whom nobody seemed to care, and after which they cared even less. What really mattered, though, is that our prophecy was fulfilled and as messengers of that exposé, sales spiked that week. And so the brief life of Rosita Canaviri, the girl child of Macusani, might not have been enough to pacify the town; but it did wonders for our print run.

At this point, it might be fitting to give a brief chronology of what went down.

A long time earlier, the Patau syndrome had delivered us an opportune arthropod, or Millipede Man; and a woman with a similar ontogenetic mutation in the low-lands of Callango, Vivian, the Three-breasted Woman, whom Atanasio found by accident once in a roadside shack, surprised to find she was single and exercising a noble profession.

Genoveva Yauri's use of Thalomide gave birth to a little Praying Mantis. Rebecca, she of the dainty stumps, barely smiled when Balbín regarded her through the camera lens before pressing the shutter. Gerald's syndactyly incident became a celebrated story that lasted for weeks, bringing him fame in the jungle as a Yucuruna because of the webbed soft tissue in all his extremities. We knew we were onto something serious when he agreed to be photographed beside a tortoise shell. Proof came a week later when he was almost lynched by a mob of Christians on the shore of a canal. We had become the town's newspaper.

Before that suffocating summer of 1992, the Karsch-Neugebauer syndrome gave us exceptionally, two human shrimps; the Aicardi syndrome the mysterious Cat Girl of Gangaylla; and the Sotos the Baby Hippopotamus of Santillana.

But I can't really say how it all got started. Or if it was as extraordinary as it seems. What I do know is that from that afternoon on, Balbín swore it was the beginning of a blessed fertility, and his version of the story was so convincing that over time the rest of us just accepted it as the truth. But things really took off when he photographed a family reunion, and said: he could always find something like a birthmark, a nail, a toe, or skull size. Weren't we all at least a little bit mutant? Who could boast normal proportions, if even Marilyn Monroe hid a six-toed left foot? We laughed when "Little Monkey" Aguilar made a lewd remark about Balbín's reputation as a womanizer, but when the laughter died away, something remained. All Balbín needed was to scrape away the sediment of laughter to find the idea.

After that, we came up with others. We had so many by the end of the afternoon that we wrote five headlines straight, and used them opportunely when we needed. It wasn't hard to find the first prodigy (Atanasio had warned us, intelligently, about the political backlash of using a word like *monster*); and when the season emptied of them, we resolved it by hitting the old archives that Balbín located and we unearthed in areas of the country that few people later cared to identify let alone imagine.

Our secret was fairly simple: we proclaimed the end of the world. Each time we found a deformity worth making public, it immediately became the sign of an earthquake, a flood, a small but imminent natural disaster. At times we only revealed something that had already taken place. At times they were merely old seeds fallen on bad earth or birthed at the wrong time.

Tracking the apocalypse, presaging the clinical deformities, seemed to fit the profile of the reader we'd already seduced and exhausted with our excesses. We too were getting tired of exploiting the aphrodisiac properties of tuberculars, or the prophecies of San Malaquías and UFO sightings, which seemed more like little scratches in whatever impossible sky, and whose occasional acts of voyeurism didn't seem to come as a surprise anymore. People imagined aliens existed but didn't want to be seen and preferred to withdraw into a kind of privacy or stubborn scrupulousness that was unnecessary if not merely boring, like any courtly, fussy love into whose arms nobody really cared to swoon.

When Benavente sent us his report from the high Andean plateau, we had been selling covers and monsters for a few months already: the Tree Man, the Crab Woman, the Mermaid Girl, the Three-headed Man of Muyuque. Atanasio's imagination never went dry. Neither did ours. But Benavente pushed the detective angle, for which fifteen years of schooling in police precincts had trained him well; and we agreed that the girl from the high-plateau's truth went beyond the supernatural nerve of the natural world. Balbín shot some great photos and two days later, having no doubt whatsoever regarding our function in the world, we went to press. It all grew from there. Every night we competed to find the sharpest headline; every morning we gave people the promise of destruction with a kind of prophetic relief. Starting with Atanasio and ending with me, the whole spectacle of ingenuity brought us a sense of purpose, made us better citizens. It's true, we became influential. The news of a kidnapping paled in comparison to a slum kid with too many limbs; the price of oil and army crusades were anesthetized if a baby's gland exploded or the bunion on a foot grew out of all proportion. People were happy to know that the world was full of ugliness, imperfection and vice. And their un-happiness was due to factors outside of their control. As long as the statistics removed them from it, we fulfilled our function: go ahead, feel at ease with this grand de-formed body that is the world.

4.

Corpus. Greek for *karpos.* Fruit. I removed my spectacles and before me I saw a single piece of glass. Eyes. In the eyes, the irises. And in the irises, the pupil. That black hole contracts invisibly. It dilates as if it were a drop re-turning to a quiet, shivering puddle. It retracts like a mus-cle. Returns to its size. Like myopia, when the lenses ad-just and the world goes back to having the same distance, the same color, the numinous vapor of failed refraction becomes liquid and the body reincorporates it, and my face responds to a name. And again the morning, in the glass that observes me, washes the water that awakens me. And I wake up.

5.

I had been eating rice in a deep dish for two days, drained by the heat of my ulcers, when I recalled the Girl-child of Sullana, née Evangelina Llocto. I had been thinking of

her before I fell asleep that night; the buddies had orga-
nized a party and someone, maybe it was Valverde, said
that Northern currents would bring flooding and a lack
of shoaling fish. I was barely awake the next day when I
perceived she was still with me. She tugged at my pajama
bottoms with the steady hand of someone fishing, and
when I looked down, I saw her combing the bathroom
tiles with her arms. Beside her was the snot-nosed boy,
sucking his fingers.

"Alright," I told them.

The girl arrived at the city hospital on the twentieth
of March, after the Ministry, sensitive to the civil campaign our newspaper had spearheaded, quickly boarded
her and her family into a van which kicked up some dust
along the way, and a bit of a scandal. A few days later,
we substituted the news of Aquilino, the leprotic Ca-
manejan, for another story. In the time it would take for
them to send a retiree back home, the doctors had photographed Evangelina's intact limbs, now stretched before
Balbín's camera like mollusks or fish just freshly out of
the water. We considered the campaign a success and the
management congratulated us. The minister promised
the mother a pension and a scholarship for the *future* girl.
All settled, everything would now follow its course, we
thought. I slept all through those nights; and in a gesture
of thanks, the girl's mother gave me a little silver chain as
a gift, which had belonged to her grandmother. But science, despite our best intentions, isn't nearly as lucrative

as superstition. Extirpating Evangelina Llocto's residual limbs didn't attract similar levels of enthusiasm from our readers; and in a quick overview I verified the fact one afternoon with my own eyes; we were only able to attract the attention of people who were unsympathetic. The truth is, our covers in the kiosks were blistering in the sun and not a single hand was coming to their rescue.

A few days later, everything back to normal, we abandoned the girl to her habitual state of anonymity.

There seemed to be a general feeling of disenchantment over the following days, as if people were unbelievably disappointed that the universal nothingness hadn't destroyed us. I walked around the streets that afternoon and couldn't rid myself of the idea: it clung like an extension of my own body.

With the Monday tumult, I couldn't help thinking how the end of the world had never ended so quickly, and the idea of a serene world, situated in the truth of its imperfection—nothing more than the frivolous ordinariness of how the people around me went about their daily lives—ended up crushing me in such an organic way that I was overcome by a dirty, gummy nausea that couldn't seem to find a way out of my body.

That's when I found the old man. I saw him sitting on a bench at the edge of the park. I always noticed people like him: old men filling out crossword puzzles not so much as a challenge to their intellect as to deposit them in our newspaper's mailbox in the hopes of winning some prize. I usually just walked by, or didn't bother to pay attention to them. But I looked at him, and he seemed to expect that I would; he clucked his tongue so I would hear it, and when I did, he looked at me over the top of his newspaper and pointed at it with a stiff, dark, cigar of a finger.

"You're the one who collects monsters," he said.

It was my newspaper he was pointing at, and I smiled, the way you smile at an accident. That old, toothless man, grinning at me as if he knew me, was just another part of the landscape, his sense of familiarity didn't bother me, I was just passing by and so I returned the courtesy. I tipped my cap and continued on my way.

"I don't believe you're announcing the end of the world," the old man said in a twang, now up and trotting steadily at my side. "Monsters. I don't think they're signs of anything."

I nodded and didn't stop this time, either.

"Hear what I'm saying, *Señor*?" he grasped my arm. "I don't think they're signs of anything."

A long time ago, I decided never to trust the people who stopped me on the street or sent letters selling the story of some deformed relative or pet. I imagined that's what he was after, so I tried to discourage him now with a less friendly smile, but the old man lost himself in his explanation, murmuring, shaking his head, and I let him keep up with me, if only not to feel invisible.

"A person can be tempted to believe in some essential rottenness that infects the world and deforms human beings," he looked as if calculating the effect of his words. "But that's not how it goes. Would you like to hear my theory?"

"Sure," I said. "Why not?"

I figured it'd take all of fifteen minutes for him to get bored with following me around. Ten more and I'd be sitting at my table in the shade, sipping a cold beer. It was early April and the sunshine still had a sting to it. Those were odd years, when everything was in flux. It was a fifteen-minute walk to La Pinta, the restaurant Half-breed Prieto had set up on a corner of Miró Quesada, where people from the newspaper met for lunch once or twice a week to exchange story ideas. Fifteen minutes, I told myself, thinking how his voice, the old man's voice, was beginning to move in and out of the din of downtown, all the hustle and bustle, the panting cars stuck in traffic and the dry cough of their nagging horns, his voice melding with the invisible buzz of routine in the air around us. But sixteen minutes later, we were still walking.

The old man said something along the road like that we should get a bite to eat, avoid the demonstrations and the police blockade that circled his *barrio*, but I didn't hear him; my stomach was starting to growl and it became a nuisance trying to listen to the both of them. The afternoon, I realized, was getting too long to share. My head suddenly seemed so heavy, and as a pleasantry, I fibbed. "I have an appointment in a half hour."

The old man looked at me with a puzzled expression, because I had also stopped in my tracks when I said it. Or maybe it was my body that stopped me, and I hadn't tried to resist its authority. I could tell how unconvincing my lie was when the old man brought a hand to his eyes, concealing them as if to dry a few tears; I've often thought that perhaps everything that happened afterwards was merely a result of my feeling guilty at being caught in a lie.

"I agree," he said, and I saw that he had started to cry. "But please understand, we should continue. What I want to show you isn't just another thing. I want you to see my son. He's at home. Five blocks. Please don't tell me you won't come."

Five blocks later, I was still following him.

"You're pale as starch," Balbín told me three hours later, when he saw me walk into the newspaper's office.

It must have been because of my bewildered expression that he became chummy, as if wanting in on the scoop.

"They call it illumination," he teased, now leaning over my cubicle. "They used to employ an emulsion of colored starch for black and white film. You know, to give color to the photos. Sometimes they painted over the photo-graphic plate, sometimes the negative or the photograph itself. The artisans were called illuminators. But as you caught yourself, the process was more sensitive to green, orange and violet. That's why the photos feel artificial. The faces look like paintings, not photos."

"Shit, Balbín," I said impatiently. "Why the photography lesson?

"Don't think I didn't see you," he said, not losing his cool, "over in that apartment in Sullana. How you stared at the photo of those old folks.

I shook my head, annoyed, and studied my desk looking for something I didn't know how to find.

"Just thought you'd want to know."

We shared an uncomfortable moment of silence, like the hangover of a bad practical joke.

"It's like when they put make-up on a dead person," Balbín said, calculating the effect of his words. "Kind of morbid, don't you think?"

"Yes," the old man said. "This way."

We must have taken a different route from the one I knew, because Ayacucho Street cut us off a long way before we reached its first corner. Farther down the street was a bare-chested man dabbing his face with vinegar to offset the tear gas that was making him cry. A few women hiding out in stores remarked behind their handkerchiefs on the locations where the bombs had gone off; stores had pulled down their metal fences awaiting the end of the protests and its lingering, noisy wake to subside, like a chord bouncing on water, and now it was less and less about finding safe places to hide out and watch firsthand the news that would be aired about their *barrios* later that afternoon, and more and more about finding detours, and the gray chaos and stink of that afternoon, the cloying sweetness like something burnt at the bottom of a pot. One grows accustomed to this and to a lot worse, the old man said: shoot, don't get me started, Señor. That's when the people stopped running.

By the time the leaden skull of the city was staring us down from a new street corner, the air had cleared up. The sky, like the open palm of a giant too rational to feel compassion, had bled its color little by little, and moved so slowly now that it seemed dead.

"Wait here," the old man said.

On the corner, I caught a glimpse of the organ grinder and his monkey just as the old man started walking, and he signaled the ridiculous pair who were taking up space on the street; I saw him negotiate with the man and wave me over.

When I got there, the organ grinder had already cranked the handlebar and the cylinder hidden in the wooden box broke out such a clunky, old-fashioned melody you could almost hear the rust. We had been on Calle Paruro when we first saw him. Now both of us, the old man and me, were there in front of the organ, in front of the organ grinder and the monkey who tendered luck, listening to their music and waiting for the absurd ritual to end.

He had said yes before, "Do you want to recall the future?"

And that's how the music of that future was playing now: in fits and starts, scaling from some nether place, or somewhere far away.

"Walter will tell you your fortune," the organ grinder said once he had me in reach. "Of course he will. But first the music has to stop sounding. Sometimes it takes a minute, sometimes twenty seconds. Who knows? Everything depends on the handlebar. So many years and it's still a mystery."

Meanwhile, the old man hugged the organ box below his shoulder, under the floating plastic that was already a little worn out, like the music.

"Strange," he said, without looking at me. "To observe objects while they rust. Sometimes it happens quickly, like when you light a flame. Things burn, the aging process accelerates, we force them to live. Sometimes, on the other hand, the process moves more slowly, like when you breathe and expel the energy that's rusting you on the inside, which dilutes in the air and nobody sees it."

"But who wants to see the future?" the organ grinder asked again. "Walter hardly works; people decide for themselves whether to come or not: nobody forces them, and let me tell you something else, the pure truth, I won't say no if they want to pay me, understand?"

"The rusting process forces objects to look for their original state," the old man said.

"And it's been a while since you've wanted to rest," the organ grinder said. "What do you say to that, Walter?"

I looked at both sides of the same face, and every once snuck a peak at the monkey.

"We all travel backwards," the old man said.

And these were the last words I heard him say before the first dizzy spell came on.

"Enough," I babbled. "Goddamit."

The monkey was small and wore a red vest with golden buttons stuck to its bony hide like a second skin that had never been acquainted with water. It could barely keep pace with the music, mimicking a sort of poorly disguised comical felicity, dancing and contorting its body as if it was either bored or intensely excited. I'm not sure how many times it repeated the performance, several, six or seven maybe, following each rotation of the organ grinder's handlebar, churning out that childhood melody from inside the box. Finally, the monkey let out an uncanny yawp and skipped out what appeared to be some sort of tempo, a simulacrum of something that had once inhabited its body but that now escaped, as if a kind of domestic humanity were being lost forever and I was bearing witness. I thought about the sound of combustion when the music stopped and the monkey salvaged a yellow card and gave it to me. Squeezing a plastic cup in its other little hand, it claimed a value for the slapdash destiny it'd just cast in my fingers.

I took out a coin and without thinking, dropped it in the cup.

Luck is written in your nature like a law inherited from your ancestors. Tremble no longer. Boundless power to fight and vanquish is within you. You can make of your life a glory or a hell: cursed be your own creature the distance that separates us from the creator. Yay the closer you come the stronger you will feel, more secure, gladder. Do the test in practical exercises every day and at the end of one, you will thank me because you'll have gained much.

I didn't know whether to laugh or lose it over that Baroque, mystical, falsely sentimental composition; all I know is that after reading it, I felt like venting to the old man.

"So now what?" I asked him. "You going to preach the gospel now? Fatima's last prophesy? The fifth finger of Santa Rosa de Lima?"

I thought my sarcasm would offend the man, whom I imagined was Catholic; and so by saying this, maybe, with an edge in my voice, might just get me off the hook. I don't think I really meant to do it, but the dancing monkey awash in filth, and the sour air of the protests had taken me to the limit of my patience and I wasn't willing to be mistreated again. I was ready to take off, but I didn't: on the contrary, it was the old man's face and not his answer that ended up deflecting my own embarrassment.

"I don't believe in God, sir."

"Yeah, morbid," I said.

Balbín was about to leave, but I called him back and asked him to sign up to take a few photos for a new headline. I don't know why I did it. I mean, why I thought about that boy. Thought, too, about the monkey's words. And what, for lack of other languages, the deformed children were trying to tell us. It might sound ridiculous, but that's what happened. After all that time, I began believing in what I was doing.

"Let Mora drive," I said.

But Balbín didn't hear me.

That's more or less how all this got started.

6.

The street he acknowledged as his own was old and in poor condition. Old, a bit rutted, but not particularly unusual. The pavement had erupted from the sidewalk that bordered his residence as if something underneath were trying to get out. I didn't find it strange. I mean, this *barrio*, the house, his home. In a way, I thought it was right for things to be like this; and that, given the exact geometry of his story and the space in which it was contained, the old man wasn't lying to me. Reaching this conclusion had a profound effect on me. At that time, I wasn't expecting to be surprised; all I wanted was to fit things into their proper molds. That's when he acknowledged a fence and asked me to follow him through a set of open bars till we were beset by an ochre-colored dwelling. The place brushed up against our legs like a dog looking for shelter; maybe that's why I felt so comfortable there, and why this new impression was another reason that made me believe he wasn't lying. I watched him take out a gray key and eagerly introduce it in a lock. I saw it turn and remain there inside.

"I've gotten to thinking at times," the old man said, as if meaning to eke out a few more minutes. "Seriously, I've put a lot of thought into what I'm going to show you this afternoon. Been considering it for days, weeks, months. Ever since he was born thirty years ago. Why did nature give me a son like this? What did I do wrong?"

His pulse slackened along with his voice, but finally we heard the latch click and I saw his lips scarring into a smile.

"But, the thing is," he said, "after asking all these questions I realized they weren't the right ones. It wasn't meant as a punishment, it wasn't any kind of sign, as you like to believe."

"Then what is it?"

Overcome by the open door, I wasn't surprised to hear

him. "You have to see for yourself."

For a few seconds, I thought that door wasn't going to open and that I would go home with a good excuse. But what happened was the door made a chirring sound as if it was laughing at me, and ended up opening. None of it lasted more than forty, maybe fifty seconds, but I understood. It became clear that I was going to enter this house, that I was going to sit on the sofa, and that I was going to spend the entire afternoon with him and his son. I understood. And that's exactly what happened. The same sweet, stagnant smell was waiting for me inside. The same sterile color. The same hencoop in the same darkness and hot vacuum of the corral, though now there was a slight variation that didn't multiply with exactitude the chaos unleashed by a few loose hens. Though what I realized as I was waiting there, is that nothing was missing. Everything seemed in order and apparently at peace.

So I made a first attempt to leave: but I felt his rough, eager hand clutching mine, as if I really did represent something important to him and maybe that's why I stayed put. Now I understand that I was the one who felt redeemed by that gesture and not the other way around. That's why I didn't leave, more than any other reason. I was a door for that sorrowful old man, perhaps the only door he had found open. And that's also why he didn't want me to go.

"Wait," the old man said. "I wouldn't want to be in your shoes, either, but first you have to see him. My firstborn. And then I'll explain everything. I'll explain, I'll show everything, and you'll be able to leave."

We reached the end of the house. A dog just stopped barking, the echoes of it swelling now, when the alarm beeped twice telling us that Julito Mora wasn't going to wait for us in the van this time. I heard the others at my back, as if they were waiting for something, and I felt relieved: this time, with them by my side, I would be able to see him.

"You going to knock?" Atanasio asked.

"No," I said, shaking my head.

I stared at the place where just four hours earlier the key had been introduced.

"No," I repeated.

And then I wrapped my palm around the door handle and felt it turn slowly, probing my fingers for the strength to allow that the slowness come from me.

"They just sent photos of the pawless dog," I said unenthusiastically, receiving the coffee. "And one of the machine operator's sisters-in-law offered an exclusive about one of her turkeys born with a surfeit of claws. Every day there are bodies that exceed their proportions, bodies that are missing a percentage of normalcy, bodies that diverge, mutate, mistake their own models. And there are those that never change. Bodies that stay fixed. Every day. And you want me to worry about your son? Please, just imagine for a moment the struggle of a human body to be born normal. The headline should be that we're born whole," I took a sip, hot. "We should celebrate it like a secret miracle. Or tell me, what is cancer if not just another kind of invisible monstrosity that deforms the human core? Or a virus. What are viruses if not ghostly beings, pure ghosts that float around the world waiting to possess a human cell in order to embody it and come alive? There you see them and don't see them. Every day. Perfect monsters.

I was satisfied with my explanation and thought maybe this time common sense would be enough to weaken his self-importance, the self-importance of the old father who still thinks his son, defective or not, is the only being on Earth worth being seen. All this would serve, I say, to keep him at a distance once and for all, this spectacle of unconcern that I no longer really felt. Over at the back the room I saw him tip the tea kettle and the hot squirt that was filling glass made me realize it was the just opposite. The old man returned, smiling. I didn't faze him then, and neither when I tried again later. As in everything else, of course, I was the one who was mistaken.

"Did you like the coffee?" he asked.

This time it was Atanasio who ran his hand along his

checkered pants, and when the old man came to pick up the tray and empty glasses, he stood up to help him.

"I think we can go up now," the old man said, gesturing with the same hand he had used before, to greet us. "Let me take care of these petty tasks while you go up to see him."

He pointed to the stairs that I was already familiar with, and Balbín hurried over to go up.

"At least they won't make us wait this time," he said.

"Can I lend a hand?" I asked.

"No," the old man said. "Go on up. You have to see it."

But for some reason I needed to stay with him, and I procrastinated with each step I took on the stairs, giving him sufficient time to catch up with me on the landing. That's where Atanasio, Julito Mora and Balbín were resting, lacking for nothing, before opening the boy's door.

"Nobody expected him to live beyond three months," I heard the old man say. "That's what the doctor told Alejanadrina and I when we asked. Three months, he said. From then on, it will depend on the Lord. His will be done . . . and here we are, thirty-three years later. And he's still alive."

He caressed my shoulder.

From the other side of the door I heard the soft voice of a woman. "Are you comfortable?"

I imagined Alejandrina the way I saw her earlier, sitting beside the bed, covering the still body under the sheets.

"Quite," I heard Atanasio.

"Can we open the curtains?" Balbín asked. "You know, for the photos. They don't come out well without light."

"It was the rust," the old man said, walking towards me, "not the box."

"Hallelujah," Atanasio joked.

The afternoon was feint, but the light filtered in as if it was scratching the room, and I sensed it illuminated the old woman's face.

"I wanted you to see the rust, not the box," the old man repeated.

"What's his name?" Balbín asked.

"Uriel" Alejandrina said.

"Uriel?" Balbín repeated. "What a nice name you have, champ. Is it okay if we move the sheet and get to know each other a little? Don't you want to see the camera I'm holding in my hands? Don't you want to be famous?"

"It's no use," Alejandrina sighed. "He doesn't listen."

"The rust?" I asked.

"You'll understand when you see," he said. "That's why you won't understand anything until he talks to you."

The old man accompanied me to the room and pointed to it, as if beyond it there was something that soon wouldn't belong to him: the hall was so dark that even in the light of day, the room's radiance seemed to swell the doorframe as if it meant to shatter it. The oxymoron, a dark light, was an aberrant voice, I remembered, from *aberrare*, meaning to stray or to deviate.

"He's inside," he said, touching the doorknocker. "My Alejandrina takes care of him, his friends look at him, and I will go in after you . . . go ahead now, don't be afraid."

I moved my head, as if it didn't weigh a thing.

After that, all he did was push the door for me to follow their voices.

7.

That afternoon was the first time there were tremors in the city.

In the beginning it was as if a horse were trying to buck us off. At first it was like this: the sound of an elephant stampede. Or an army tank. Tanks. And boots. Countless footfalls. A soundless sound that swelled little by little, as if someone had forgotten to plug up its source and everything there had slipped away: simply, like full water; it collected, it reached the brim, it spilled over. Then the entire Earth arched its back and the vertebrae moved one after the other like a concert of stridencies, like a terrible but smiling skeleton that shook its structure in a contradictory farce we weren't able to interpret.

I cried or celebrated, who could really know.

Thirteen hours later, when something tiny had already broken in the Earth's heart (it was the hour devoid of light), we saw the world from below. Then we saw it from on high again. And every time it returned, it was a dusty, new world, and yet an old one at the same time, but new, and every time it moved out, something emerged from its crevices, a dry space, a palpable emptiness, the swing of a reverse fold that made us feel tenderly, made us love ourselves with an urgency that was all too human and at the same time unlike anything human we'd ever known till then. (This was the hour devoid of sound). And it was as if through them, I mean, through those very crevices, no river would ever flow again, we looked at them with a species of grateful terror, as if we would never see the river that flowed through them again, or at least we would no longer be able to see it as through the same eyes.

I spent that afternoon perched on the stairs of my building, watching the stream of the vast avenue fill with people: people gathering in doorways, people crowded under awnings, people dispersed around the parks, people assembling on rooftops and balconies, people in buildings, in the uppermost vantage points, in the farthest, most out-of-the-way places in the mountains surrounding the city. People. Houses. Everything seemed new. And everything was, in a certain sense. Or not: it was merely something old that the Earth had allowed to escape. Something so old that it became new just by looking at it. People waiting for the end of the world is what I saw that afternoon. People, by and large, that's all. Seeing it, perhaps for the first time, I thought: this is something you've already seen.

That's not how we announced it that afternoon. Or what we had imagined before the whole thing got started. But we saw him. We saw him not once, but several times.

We saw him, sure, eyes clouded in tears, and we swear there was satisfaction, too. This must be the miracle everyone was talking about now: the tears that had already washed us clean inside and that divided like two open, idiot eyes that didn't know how to explain the world. I knew the instant that boy's hand touched mine and it melted like butter between his fingers that the world was destroying itself for the first time. The moment he brought that simulacrum of a mouth to my ear, and said exactly what I wanted to hear, without knowing, without being able to hear it. It wasn't only the Earth that moved as if scratching at pesky fleas, opened wide so we could see our departed, the dead ones we've buried over the years. Because we didn't want to see that. And we wouldn't see it. But the dead slipped out, stirred by the Earth's tectonic plates. And this was no longer ours alone. What was being destroyed beneath the soles of the world belonged, finally, to everyone.

Mr. Munch

For Sarah Beytelmann

MY GOOD FRIEND ERNESTO MALINSKY once said the best
way to divest of risky projects was to see them fail. That
afternoon, we both got haircuts at the barbershop downtown and that's what—our new public image, that is—
sent us out to the world with the vague cool of genuine,
parsimonious badasses. The manager of our company,
Enrique Baigorretegui, had personally mapped our route:
one that got lost—we found out later—in the tightest av-
enues of socio-economic sector B in Santa Beatriz, an old
suburb of bourgeois houses that had seen better times, if
not overrun by the sudden influx of language schools and
computer programming centers employing nobody but
their single owner. As we studied the map a few hours
earlier, scarcely paper and ink, it revealed to us a sort of
interior road. And maybe, as a result, we both left the office believing in all earnestness that the portable vacuum
cleaner *Hoffnung S314* would clean away all the setbacks
and little deprivations that marked our lives.

"Your problem, Miguelito, is that you don't know how

to be practical," Malinksy said that afternoon, five streets down.

Malinsky loved to dole out unsolicited advice. He was eager and enthusiastic, and that afternoon, though nobody had asked him to, he started sharing some of his rules for success. We had walked a long stretch, lugging the company's folding samples cases (I should add here that he lugged the little blue one and I the red one, which created a great barrier between us), and I had shared with him my plans for the future, how I was going to save up to go back to school in a few years, work in the spring for when winter comes . . . that sort of stuff: be lucky, invest in a good profession, be an ant and not a locust, etc.

I remember looking Malinsky straight in the eye when they were cutting our hair, and praising the advantages of a possible academic life. He was like a fat kid wedged on his throne wearing a huge napkin tied around his neck: from there, with that sort of transcendental gluttony, he smiled. He let me prattle on, and when I finished talking he looked at himself self-satisfied, framed in the straight, equal proportions of his kingly coif. Then he looked at me again, as if for the first time. I don't ever remember seeing him sport a hairstyle different from this one, never heard him speak in any other tone of voice. I still remember his moon-shaped face and bright eyes, his luminous laughter, so convinced of his own vigor as we stood before the door leading out to the avenue drawn on the map by our boss; that show of strength is what made me halt the

wheels of my little suitcase now even lighter of contradictions—though still red—and finally ring the first doorbell
of my life.

"If you don't believe me, consider this," he pointed out.
"Failures are the best things that can happen to you in
this life, Miguelito. If you succeed, good for you, you're
a successful guy and everyone will want to copy you.
And you'll be able to share the experience with someone, no matter who, and influence him or her. Like what
I'm doing now, eh? And if you fail"—and here he gave
me a little pat on the shoulder—"you get rid of the junk.
Goodbye failures! Tell me, what do you need them for, if
you're going to start all over again . . ."

Then he pointed to the rib of a door.

"Go ahead," he said, "press."

I pressed.

Malinsky had already lost nearly everything by then,
including his father's monthly allowance—the old man
refused to continue supporting someone incapable of giving him a grandson—a full-time job in the post office,
and the little respect his second wife, Lucinda, still had
for him. Things had gotten worse with unemployment,
but fortunately one of his brothers-in-law recommended
him for a job and I was brought in with him, in part because my mother insisted on it, and in part driven by my
own failures. At the time I thought, as I had explained to
Malinsky, that I could earn some money at Harry Teitelbaum's import business and move up the ladder quickly

if I did things the right way. How hard could it be to sell something in a country so committed to its own tolerance for corruption? If they could reelect a president who had robbed them of their dignity for nearly ten years, I told myself, why not sell the promise of a consumer electronic that at the very least would actually turn on when they flipped the switch. The company's commercial logic seemed infallible to me at the time, being a young, ambitious man, reasonably attractive, twenty-five years old. All I needed was to polish my conversation skills, dress in a smart suit, and iron my tie. Know the right doors to knock on. Or knock on them all until one, by luck or by mistake, does the trick. Malinsky's words, lubricated by his soft-shelled pessimism, never truly convinced me, though they didn't discourage me, either. I tried not to take him too seriously, anyway, especially after they shut the first doors in our faces. I tried not to again, a little while later, when the whole block's hinges had groaned and our faith began to flag. And confronted by the unspoiled rejection that followed us on our route, I began to believe, maybe in order to think about something with greater conviction, that in order to sell something in this country, you had to become a politician.

When we got back, Baigorretegui surprised us with a bear hug so crushing it was hard to disengage. He didn't care that we'd returned with every single one of the *Hoffnung S314* vacuum cleaners we'd carried out in our sample cases. We'd learn how to deal with the rejection he told us, Baigorretegui, I remember it well, patting our sweaty, sixteen kilometers-of-slammed-doors backs.

"And the day you do," he added, in a tone of voice that still gives me the shivers, "you'll become *real* men."

Two weeks later, on All Saint's Day, I found Malinsky dead, swinging by his neck from one of the highest beams in his dining room. His words took on a kind of mystic revelation to me that day, which is tough to explain. Might have been the first time I actually listened to him, aware that an essential truth had been revealed to me, at least in those few seconds in front of the barbershop mirror. I don't recall crying over him, not on the day of the funeral, not when we read his last words and testament together with some of his closest relatives, including my mother, three weeks later.

His wife, Lucinda, she had definitely had good weep.

While the lawyers enumerated Malinsky's legacy of debts (which took at least fifteen minutes), Lucinda kept scrunching her Kleenex into little balls and throwing them into the trashcan, one after the other, with perfect aim. She wore a cute little widow's get-up to inaugurate her new figure: black skirt, black blazer, black hose, black shoes. A little veiled pillbox hat, netting draped over her eyes, was all that gave color to her new personality. She was attractive, but I didn't tell her that. I stared, curious at how she was able to cry without getting her eyes wet.

* * *

One afternoon I found myself reconnoitering the walls of my room, scrutinizing them from my bed as if I might find some secret door hidden in the texture of the cement. When Malinsky died (I mean, when we eventually buried him) I knew right away it was time for me to split, but I didn't have enough money or anyone to take me in. Truth was, Lucinda didn't really mind me hanging around a few more days. Which kindled my hopes, and soon enough I found myself thinking less and less about the transit I was supposed to be arranging on my own, sooner or later. Eventually I figured the idea of leaving might even be unnecessary, and soon enough I forgot about it entirely. It was hard to imagine anyone wanting to rent the home of a suicide victim. People thought the place was stained by his death, by his indelible spirit, by something that couldn't be washed away in an everyday explanation. Shortly before she moved back in with her parents, Lucinda covered up the windows with posters and left me there alone in exchange for occasionally showing the apartment to potential renters. I was supposed to answer the phone every once in a while. A woman asked about the living room's decor. A man inquired after more practical things: expenses, repairs, hypotheticals, whether the documents were up to date. I answered everyone in a graceful and diligent manner: I talked about the constructed space, praised the interior decoration, evaluated the prime location, and listed, without the aid of notebooks, the building's community fees, policies and the monthly rent, which wasn't excessive.

I rarely mentioned my buddy Ernesto and how he'd hung himself from the highest beam in the dining room. Appointments were only granted for people who showed a little enthusiasm, and not without first warning about the uncomfortable situation that had forced down the property value. An elderly couple didn't seem too greatly perturbed, but all the others answered with a slow swelling of the lungs, like they were about to jump into a swimming pool. People in this city are superstitious. What can I say? Not a single visit, ever. The elderly couple found the location very convenient, but the flat impractical ("the elevators don't always work," I told them with my best smile), and few others bothered to ask, and few actually showed up on the day of the appointment, after engorging their lungs and hanging up the phone. Yet the memory of Malinsky began to fade as the weeks passed, like a belt that's been loosened a notch or two, and even the doorman stopped making the sign of the cross every time yet one more message arrived, a little too late to matter anymore. I lived in relative peace, though I couldn't help thinking how unfair people had been to good old Ernesto, my good friend Malinsky, who had invited me to live in his home for a while, shortly before he died.

By then I had become part of the official Baigorretegui team, so my promotion in the Teitelbaum Company no longer seemed inappropriate. They assigned me a blue drop-down sample case and that very day a sonorous round of applause propelled me out into the street, impervious to rejection and embarrassment to being under the guardianship of a *big brother*. Malinsky always said that marrying a woman from a wealthy family was a blessing and a curse. And I never understood what he meant until the day Lucinda called me at home and I listened to her unflappable, cruel voice telling me how to clear out. My only belongings were a rather unsupportive, overstuffed mattress, a few plates filched from my parents, a microwave and a little two-element camping stove that didn't need much energy to get blazing red. I packed it all into a taxi and sat next to the driver. Mr. Munch, my cat, sat purring on my lap.

And, oh, Lucinda had been a little rude that day, but she was right: the time had come for me to leave. I had lived there for ten months, two weeks, and five days on her nickel.

"Just tell me where you want to go, Maestro," the black guy behind the steering wheel said.

I had one hundred and twenty-two *soles*, and forty-four cents in my pocket. It was in something like six bills and four faded gold coins. I caressed them without tenderness or at least not with that honest kind of love that's lavished on legitimate children. It was money that wouldn't long be in my hands, and I knew it way before earning it. I enjoyed the moment, though, yes, I enjoyed these seconds of not saying a word, of not knowing anything, and smiling, slowly, I pet my cat as if he were the one I wished had time to surprise me.

"Do you have an address, sir?" the driver said finally, impatiently.

I shook my head.

On the other side of the car's windows, the world shook as if it meant to wake people up. But wake them for what end was less important. It was a lackluster day like any other, and the people filling it in disintegrated before my eyes, thousands of their fragments, parts of humanity they no longer recognized as belonging to them, lost in the back alleys of the ashen city, from whose map I wasn't able to extract a simple route. Is this what my life meant? I looked at my cat and Mr. Munch looked at me. The three of us looked at each other: Mr. Munch, the black man, and me, but the only gaze that seemed sentient, from center of a city now quiet after so much agitation, was that of my cat.

In the urgency of those seconds, the only thing I recalled was my mother's maiden name, which I said.

The driver answered smiling, "I think I know where that is."

And that's where we went.

That's how it started.

It was a bashful opening at first, the creaking door, the sleep-ridden eyes, a circumspect yawn, a breathing gill, withdrawn skin, a sigh. One sentence: Hold on, please. Then it simply closed. I heard the chain lock slide and a minute later there were the uneasy little eyes opened wide, encrusted into a compact face, distrusting, hardly kind.

In the sales and marketing training course, Baigorretegui showed us how to identify people's weaknesses. It's an ability, he said, that's nearly as important as making someone feel the need for the product you're selling.

"After all," he said, and I remember him moving back and forth in front of the blackboard like a caged tiger, "sales breed a weakness, but to make it visible, first we sell strength."

The man in front of me must have been about five foot eight from the floor to the last strand of his hair. He was dried out and white as a sheet, and didn't seem to have much of a sense of being useful.

"To begin with, take into account two facts: first, all humans have some need waiting to be met. Which one? Well, that's what we're here to figure out, gentlemen. Second, we all need acknowledgement. Our lives are full of absences. If you're able to really digest these two qualities, I promise you will be successful in developing effective sales strategies."

Baigorretegui pointed to one of the students and asked them to summarize what he just said.

"We look at their physical appearance and draw a mental map of their weaknesses," Piazze said.

"Correct," the manager nodded. "Then what?"

"If he's short and unattractive," I said, rushing to an assumption, "we should pay him a compliment . . ."

"No, no and no," Baigorretegui's face flushed. "Don't even think about it. He would feel humiliated; he would feel he's being conned, deceived by your rhetoric. If you aren't honest about his physique, which the fleshy man will pick up on in a snap (let's note that women are different on this front), how is he ever going to take the product you're offering seriously?"

I raised my hand.

"What if he doesn't need a portable vacuum cleaner? How do we know the product is suitable for a certain type of client?"

Baigorretegui paused.

"Tell me, Mr. Popiloff, and please respond frankly. We're among friends here. Would you, if you were in our targeted client's place, need a portable vacuum cleaner?"

I doubted for a second and finally responded. "I suppose not, sir."

"That's where I wanted to go," Baigorretegui's face seemed more relaxed now. "Thank you, Mr. Popiloff. Nobody in this room really needs a portable vacuum cleaner. Maybe nobody in the city needs one. Have you ever seen one in a car? In an office? In a university?"

The students laughed.

"Of course not, get me? But you see it's the most important thing there is. What's important about it is," and he picked up a piece of paper from the mountain on his desk, "'eight out of ten people in our city think pollution is the principal cause of respiratory illness.'" He picked up another, "'Nine of these same people warn that dust is as serious as humidity.' Nine out of every ten. And here comes the most important point, how can all of these fine people fight respiratory problems when we live in a city that has ninety-five percent humidity?"

A glass of water, dried in a single gulp, seemed to alleviate his sudden swoon. Baigorretegui was getting dehydrated, sweating heavily.

"At Teitelbaum, Inc., we listen to the *real* needs of our clients. Ordinary, everyday people, gentlemen. The common folk. That man, this woman, people who can't afford an electric dehumidifier. But Teitelbaum, Inc.'s salespeople go a little further: we know *how* to change people's everyday problems into business opportunities."

When Baigorretegui broke into a sweat, it always started above his upper lip.

"So, why sell gadgets that nobody uses, Mr. Popiloff?"

"Because we don't just sell products," I said, in a moment's epiphany. "We sell solutions."

I felt the pat.

"That's the right answer, gentlemen. We don't sell vacuum cleaners, we sell health."

I gave my little foldout case a squeeze. "We sell health," I answered, looking at the scrawny figure standing at the threshold of my nineteenth door, the one in front of me, the first one that didn't shut on this September morning. I felt I should clutch at it like someone who was shipwrecked, but the idea clutched me instead, as if I were a wooden plank bobbing and I were a hundreds, thousands of miles away from the shore. Faking the need to breathe, I brought my hand to my diaphragm. I breathed in theatrically, as if the air had difficulty entering my lungs, and then I smiled.

"Sorry," I said, now visibly recovered, "sometimes I think this summer humidity is going to be the death of me yet. Do you know how many buckets of water an electric dehumidifier drains every day in a fifty square-foot room?"

The man shook his head.

"Fifteen," I answered. "Twenty-two in the summer."

A plastic smile folded across his face, as if he'd been slapped.

"Tell me about it," he relaxed the leg that was leaning against the crack in the door. "I have asthma, can't you tell?"

That night I sat down to watch television with Mr. Munch on my lap. Blondie says to Tuco: "You see in this world there's two kinds of people, my friend, those with loaded guns and those who dig. You dig." Ah, Clint Eastwood, I've always loved it when he plays the cowboy: something about him reminds me of a traveling portable vacuum cleaner salesman. Mr. Munch would agree if only he could see me out there, kicking up the dust. And that swagger. But I was on edge that night; maybe that's why I wanted Mr. Munch's feedback when the last commercial break came on, as if this time he could actually talk. It's really not so strange, I told myself, that a man have a conversation with his cat of a Saturday night. It was only a skip and a song from there to asking him why Malinsky had hung himself. The question had been going round and round in my mind, relentless as an old cowboy since the afternoon I found him swinging from the dining room beam. Over and over again, I tried to understand Ernesto's decision, and time and time again, always whisperingly, I ended up at the same detour sign. What would bring such a vigorous man, someone so enthusiastic about life, to do away with himself? And why when he was about to get the promotion we all figured was imminent? Hard to imagine. And every time I tried, my eyes would move and the image in my head disappeared. Mr. Munch alone knew the truth about Malinsky's last breaths on earth. My house was his house since the day I showed up at the Malinsky's, suitcases in hand, and I could imagine him slinking around the chairs, observing through those unsettling, dilated yellow eyes as Ernesto removed his shoes and arranged the high-backed chair just below the beam, tied the chord with a good, proper knot, and took that last, categorical step, one fell swoop into the void. The lizard-like spasms probably startled him, but he was curious: each time I imagined him there, looking up at Ernesto in the heights, I noticed a kind of inappropriate inquisitiveness in his feline features. Oh yeah, did I ever know my cat. He'd never have deserted him while he shuddered, while that perfectly tied chord crushed Malinky's neck squeezing the last drop of life from him, my little pussycat would have smoothed along, lurking below his convulsing socks, under his peaceful socks.

Shame, anyway, that Mr. Munch can't speak.

"You're mistaken," he responded.

I opened my eyes and looked at him, shocked. I couldn't deny for the past eight years Mr. Munch had always given signs of being exceptionally intelligent and discreet. Hearing him speak at long last, I think I asked myself if it wasn't like the case of those proverbial monkeys who it's said didn't speak because they didn't want to be put to work.

"How am I mistaken?" I asked, watching him lick a paw and suddenly, as if it were an opposing action, I stopped petting his back.

"In so many ways," Mr. Munch said. "To start with, Malinsky didn't commit suicide."

I jumped up.

"You mean he was murdered?"

Mr. Munch clicked his tongue.

"What I mean is that he didn't kill himself alone."

I grabbed the cat and brought him close to my face.

"Speak clearly, *Cheshire!*"

But his body was too supple, and too slippery for my trembling hands and he dropped to the floor on all four paws, where he quickly scurried away. Though I spent the rest of the evening trying to extract more information from him, Mr. Munch seemed to have recovered the convenience of his meows and didn't come near the sofa till I had switched off the television and went to bed with a vague feeling of failure and guilt. Before I fell asleep, though, I heard him lapping up his milk and suspected that he had me under surveillance from some hiding place.

Every April 26, Mr. Harry Teitelbaum traveled from his Coral Gable residence in Miami to inspect for himself his business interests scattered over this part of the southern hemisphere. Baigorretegui quaked in his shoes for fifteen minutes, and by the time he was finished, the great boss's jubilant welcome was ready.

It took some effort but we pooled some funds into a little kitty, and the following weekend, just before Mr. Teitelbaum's visit, we completed the office renovation. The receptionists sported brand new uniforms, our salesmen had visited the barber, and the walls were decorated with images that supported our cause and all the motivational phrases we could come up with.

When Baigorretegui walked out of his office, someone whistled at him (he was dressed in a bow tie and corduroy jacket), but instead of getting angry he bowed his head in acknowledgement and we all applauded, our spirits soaring before his good humor. That night we met in the motivational room (Baigorretegui called it *Circe's Salon*) and amid bouts of song and blazing rhetoric, together we pledged that when the big boss arrived he should find if not the most profitable branch in all of the southern hemisphere, at least the most inspired and hands-on of them all.

"*I like this,*" the rubicund old man said as he walked in the door.

Baigorretegui brought him by the arm to our main room, where we sang him a bilingual song we'd been practicing for a while. We fumbled through, tapping the beat out on our notebooks, hugging each other between robust ovations until someone finally recited the finale poem that spoke of brotherhood and eternal duty. When it was over, Mr. Teitelbaum made a sound with the palms of his hands and left us trapped in a silence that beat like an arm that was held under a tight grip and then suddenly freed.

"Thanks for your enthusiasm, ladies and gentlemen," he said in English.

"*El señor Teitelbaum agradedece a todos su entusiasmo,*" Baigorretegui quickly translated.

"This is the first place in Latin America where I've felt like I was in the First World," the old man laughed.

Baigorretegui succumbed to a sudden fit of laughter, and the rest of us echoed him.

"He feels at home," he added, humbly, though we knew he recognized his own vanity.

We applauded.

Mr. Harry Teitelbaum grabbed the microphone tightly and now paced before the white board exuding self-confidence. He was a burly man, broad-shouldered, and with facial features as resolute as his movements.

"*We have a mission here, gentlemen.*" He started to sweat, he spat, he walked to and fro. "*Believe it or not, most people think capitalism has only empty, selfish aims. But, in the name of our God, I tell you our mission on Earth is not merely to satisfy the needs of mankind, giving people material satisfaction. We all carry our Lord's Testimony throughout our efforts, love and sincere dedication to our jobs. Have no doubt about your commitment in this beloved and suffered country, gentlemen. Thank you from the bottom of my heart, I am very proud of the modern evangelization that you are carrying out.*"

It didn't much matter that we couldn't understand a single word he said. Before Baigorretegui had even started to translate, those of us seated in the back shouted "bravo," and it didn't take long for the sharp, hurried applause to run through us like a wave.

This lasted two minutes and slowly faded away, I mean, as our sales manager calmed the furor, motioning with his hands up and down, like a couple of fans.

"Great, ladies and gentlemen," he said, "gentlemen, please, on behalf of Mr. Teitelbaum, here with us now, I want to thank you all, thank you for your professionalism and teamwork. You heard what he had to say. This was a very pleasant visit. *Una visita muy placentera.* Now, let's go out into the streets, *señores,* and begin our mission, not without one last word of congratulations from our Great Big Brother, an extraordinary inspiration for the young company we have the pleasure of honoring with our daily labor. Three hurrahs for Mr. Teitelbaum, ladies and gentlemen! Hip, hip!"

"Rah, rah, raaaah!" we all responded in a single voice.

"I can't hear you people!" Baigorretegui insisted, raising his arms, drying the tears in his eyes. "Come on now, like one single voice . . . like one single company!"

That night I had a dream. I was strolling alone down a long beach, marbled with deep grooves like the wrinkles on an old person's face, expressing something like worry or wisdom. The beach was a lot bigger than normal, at least it seemed as much in my dream; I walked along until I came to a fork in the path. It was getting dark and I could feel something rubbing against my left calf, something warm, familiar, and pleasant. I looked down. It was Mr. Munch.

"Since you think you're such a smart cat," I stopped him, looking straight into his eyes, "which path should we take now?"

"That depends on where you want it to lead you," he answered.

"Very far," I said.

The verses we sang every morning during our motivational exercises popped into my mind:

Traveler, your footsteps
are the path, and nothing more;
Traveler, there is no path,
the path is made by walking.

Then I heard myself repeating the verse aloud. "Traveler, there is no path, the path is made by walking."

Mr. Munch shook his head. "That depends on who is walking."

I looked at my watch and it was just a little before six, and the morning sky was tinged with red. Light filtered in through the windows of the old building, scratching through the lace curtains. I looked out through the same windows, through the slit that had been left open, the sharp eye that also opened, slowly, and I thought I saw a pair of distinguished gentlemen walking at the edge of a trail. They were dressed in frock coats and top hats. They moved into the distance with a slow gait I would never have been able to keep up with, and suddenly I felt exhausted by the imperative of so much elegance. So I crossed my legs and allowed myself to fall back onto the armchair.

"Look at this card," I told Mr. Munch.

"The hangman," the cat observed.

"It's an interesting one," I added. "We live in a state of repose where external factors are always chipping away at us. We should accept our destiny and sacrifice some-thing in exchange. It's time to clean our conscience, re-flect on how we are, what we do, why we do it and how we do it, before *the moment* arrives."

"But you're upside-down," Mr. Munch said. "Con-trariwise, you'd be head-first."

I looked at the rug; there was a rope tied around one of my feet.

"That modifies the meaning," I nodded.

"Lack of sacrifice, great difficulties or obstacles, disin-terest, waning willpower, incapacity for dedication, de-lays in making plans, aborted projects, unfulfilled promis-es, impotence, insensitivity, worry for oneself, unjustified martyrdom, useless sacrifice, circulatory problems."

"I don't have circulatory problems," I interrupted, piqued. "I'm very aware of where I want to go. If I walk enough, I'll get somewhere; but that doesn't matter, as long as I go far."

"In that case," Mr. Munch said, "it doesn't matter what direction you take."

I thought a moment.

"What time is it?"

I'd been hearing the clock's pendulum swinging to and fro for a few minutes; it was like a Ping-Pong game, only I couldn't see what was invisible. I looked for Mr. Munch then, tired by the absence of the ball game, and saw him transformed into a wall clock hanging on a green post that at the same time looked like it was losing its color, or melting. His tail was straight and his body glowed blue, as if it had been shined with wax. From left to right and then (he moved his eyes) from right to left and then again from left to right and on and on until I stopped following.

"Now you're useful in ways you weren't before," I told him.

"I always have been," he answered. "You just never bothered to notice."

My head hurt too much to answer, and though I did, he must have noticed because he asked me shortly, "How do you cut a man's head off when he doesn't have a body?"

I knew it was a riddle, but the pendulum that he was now, swung more and more fervently and time began coiling, making spirals, sinking in without penetrating anything, as if it were a streamer flung vertically over the ground at the end of a party.

"Malinsky," I said to myself, not knowing very well why.

His eyes came to a halt in the center. I knew then, perhaps trapped by some old regret, the path I should follow was there.

"Aha," Mr. Munch said, all tooth and smiles now. "Malinksy."

Malinsky, I repeated, and moving my head as if someone else were shaking it, I woke up in a sweat.

Someone rang the doorbell so gingerly, so pitiably, caressing it *tintinnabulatingly* that at first I didn't realize the individual—whoever it was—had been waiting there some four minutes for me to open the door. I approached, rubbing my eyes, now sullied again by the daylight. Lucinda's face was bulging through the peephole, giving her a huge, Groucho Marx nose, making her look utterly ridiculous. When I opened the door, everything fell back into order like the sweep of an accordion swallowing its own sound. She was back to being beautiful again, and I repressed a spasm of admiration, once again the mere spectator who had always been by her side. It used to happen often, every time Malinsky and I came back from work. I'd imagine it was me she kissed, stretching out on the sofa, it was to me she served the best plate at dinner, to me she made love in the darkness of the next room, stifling a slow and satisfying orgasm that I tried to imitate later when I masturbated alone on the sofa. It was hard for me to look her in the eyes without feeling that sharp pinch in my heart, but Mr. Munch was there to meow at me and take advantage of the confusion Lucinda's presence brought, and sneak off into the kitchen somewhere. I took me a second to realize, though, that Lucinda was holding him when she walked in. I was stunned, and she seemed able to gauge my reaction.

"I found him at home," she said, brushing her sweat suit as if trying to get rid of invisible feline traces. "At least fifteen blocks from here. I walked out into the yard to get some exercise and there he was, dying of thirst poor thing."

I heard Mr. Munch lapping at his plate.

"He was dying of thirst the poor thing, so I brought him home," she repeated. "I knew he belonged to you. Don't you think it's strange?"

I nodded.

"Who knows how a cat's memory works?" I said, trying to make little of it.

"A little better than some of the men I know."

I smiled.

"I've been promoted a few times at work," I invited her to come on in. "You'd be surprised how far I've moved up since I started. Why don't you stay for a coffee or something and I'll tell you about it."

"Gustavo already told me," she said, reminding me her brother was a manager. "But I'll take you up on the drink—just for a little bit. It's been a while since we've caught up."

She made herself comfortable and I went for a cup of tea and some cookies.

I poured the hot water and dunked a little teabag until the bottom of the ceramic cup filled with a soft earthen color.

She looked at me when I came back in.

"So how've you been, stranger?"

I guess she must have come for this. To "stranger" me. To her, I'd always been Malinsky's little shadow, an oblique, irregular extension of him. I mean I was still young, and in some way to Lucinda it meant that there was a lasting bond between us, since just like her, I expected to live in this world for a long time still. That continuity, the unseen traces of habits that remain long after an apartment is auctioned or a debt cancelled, long after photographs are ripped apart in the autumnal tremble of a hand or clothes packed into boxes and set on fire, traces cannot be washed away on their own, and something must have happened because when Lucinda saw me this new way, living in a different house, I became another person to her, someone detached from Malinsky, from the person I was with Malinsky, and these were the only circumstances that allowed me to understand that Lucinda had come not only to "stranger" me, but also to bury him, to throw a handful of earth on that unseen, dead body that the two of us together represented, burying us, in her eyes, once and for all.

Maybe that's the only reason I dared to say, "I dreamt of Ernesto yesterday."

Lucinda stretched across the sofa and I felt as if, seven months after his death, something of Malinsky's was beginning to surface.

"Anything special?"

"I think he was hanging," I said, and if that wasn't enough, I added, "and so was I."

"It's not the same thing to dream that you're hanging as to see a hangman in your dream," she said. "You know?"

I shook my head no.

"Following Ernesto's death, I've had a lot of time to

think, to waste time, as you can see, reading silly esoteric literature."

"That makes two of us," I said. "I even have conversations with my cat."

Mr. Munch had opportunely appeared beside the rug and feeling the connection we have sometimes, looking at each other, Lucinda and I laughed.

"It's so nice to see you again."

***

"The manager is calling for you," Carmen said, approaching the drawer where I kept my shirts.

She looked absorbed, as if she were hiding something, and added, "It seems important, Miguelito."

More than what she said, it was Carmen's tone of voice that irritated me. Rumors about staff reductions had been going round a few months earlier, which Mr. Teitelbaum's visit had luckily helped to dispel. People now worked with a greater sense of security, believing this could be a lifelong business. By now I hardly remembered I'd had dreams of going to college, and often thought by way of justification that I was an ant that no longer aspired becoming a cicada. Truth be told, I had raised my productivity and that gave me a certain edge. In August alone my sales percentage was nearly sixty-three percent more than the first trimester. That and a recent bonus for the increasing fidelity of my portfolio allowed me to knock on Baigorretegui's door calmly, though I'd already figured that I couldn't expect anything from the people you see every day. Today they're giving you an honest piece of advice, and tomorrow they're hanging you from the highest beam.

"Come on in," I heard him say.

The manager pointed to the chair and I sat down.

"You remind me of myself when I was your age," Baigorretegui said as soon as he saw me. "You belong to a certain class of dreamers, of poets. Salespeople often think of this as a mundane job, just public relations, a few pats on the back and nothing more." He lit a cigarette and for the first time I saw him smoking, reclining heavily in his chair. "But truth is, Miguelito, selling is an art. An art," he relished the smoke of his phrase, "which needs a special kind of sensitivity, a poetic gift of imagination and word."

A mouthful of smoke formed a ring that evaporated just as quickly.

"I know you understand what I'm getting at."

"Of course, Mr. Baigorretegui," I said.

"Please, call me Enrique," he said, clicking his tongue. When you come through that door," he signaled it, "there are no more differences, no hierarchies between us. It's company policy."

"Enrique," I smiled.

"That's the way I like it," the manager said. "And that's why I like you. Imagine. I've been following you since you came in with Malinsky (may he rest in peace), and I never stopped seeing myself in you from day one. Restless, motivated, enthusiastic." He pulled a document out of his drawer in a solemn, practiced movement. "I have your six-month performance results and if I may, Miguelito, it's nothing short of an Andean slope."

He laughed.

"You've climbed Salkantay, Miguelito."

"Thanks," I said, truly appreciative. "All I can say, Enrique, respectfully, is that it's all thanks to your coaching."

Baigorretegui blushed.

"That's another thing I truly value in people like you, Miguelito. Modesty."

He flicked his ashes into a curvy dish festooned with stripes that looked like zebra hide. His eyes surveyed the little pile of ashes he'd left, evaluated it and then, suddenly, squashed it.

"Because, to be honest, the world is full of envy, of traitors, of selfish, mediocre people, Miguel. I'm not saying anything new," he smiled. "Even at Teitelbaum, Inc. What do you think of that? Even here there are Cains among brothers. There are felons in all of this," and his hand moved towards the wooden door as if to pass right through it, "among the multitude we live with every day. How does that strike you? Turn your back and watch out for the stones they're throwing."

"I'd never believe it if it weren't coming from you," I encouraged him.

"Oh, yes, believe it, believe it," he brought a hand to his forehead and rubbed a little, musing for a few seconds. "But the Lord's will prevails. Look at this right here," he said, showing me a letter written on company's letterhead. I saw his fingers grab the pencil and a quick stroke slide over his name: my new position. "Mr. Harry asked me personally to oversee the new branch our company's opening in Santa Cruz, Bolivia. What do you think about that, Miguelito? Enrique Baigorretegui, pioneer for the institutional future in unknown territory. Who'd have thought? What an honor! What a show of support! What a blow for all my haters hiding in the shadows!"

He moved his body forward, wide, elegant, a creature of the morning, and I saw his eyes alighting on me like a pale fire.

"And this other one," Baigorretegui said, sliding a similar document forward, softly grazing my fingers, "is the second most important decision I'm making for the company."

I followed his gaze, serene now, to its endpoint, and recognized my own name printed in letters on a white void full of potential.

"I've always been a man of instincts and I know that with you, Miguel Jacobo Popiloff, I'm not mistaken."

He moved the pen towards me.

"Sign," he said, "and my post belongs to you."

* * *

Three months later we arranged to meet in a café in San Isidro. I preferred to sit out on the patio because it was a sunny day. And because I intuited, an hour before our appointment, that I should be seated and she should be standing. I gazed at the buildings shored up along the street. A Turkish bath announced in tight blue lettering projected shadows on a group of bankers who took their time going in. I also watched the passionless traffic of an early March afternoon and three lanes of parked cars whose silvery aluminum finishes gleamed like open chocolate wrappers.

"This is very weird," Lucinda said, by way of a welcome.

"What's so strange about you and I meeting for a cup of coffee?" I said jokingly. "Am I that ugly and ridiculous to you?"

I stood up when I saw her.

"All I'm saying is that it's strange of you to invite me to such a swanky place, Miguelito."

I had no way of dispossessing her of her suspicion. Fifteen months ago she would have had to pick up the tab herself.

"Things are different now," I said.

The waiter handed me the menu and I stroked its supple, leathery surface, knowing that Lucinda was in front of me, eyeballing me. With time I've learned how to decipher certain messages women drizzle around in their encounters with men. I mean things like playing with their hair, fixing their earrings, needlessly smoothing their skirt. They seduce any surface in their vicinity in a dactyl manner. And contrary to that, I remain still; I watch them knowing these tactile sensations to be my own, I smile as if I were interested in something inanimate that is not her. The menu, for example.

"How about fig cheesecake?" I point to the flirty typography with my finger, gluttonously bent towards the paper.

"If it comes with a cappuccino, I accept," she said.

"You heard the lady," I raised my eyes and looked straight into the waiter's pupils. "And I'll have a double espresso."

The waiter bowed and retired.

It was my first victory of the day. I realized that I hadn't said please yet and that, in fact, I had wanted to.

"Looks like you don't plan on getting any sleep tonight," Lucinda said, without hiding her smile.

I couldn't resist.

"That depends on you."

Lucinda let out a squeal and I smiled as I contemplated the corresponding relation between the echo of my sentence and her equally spontaneous response.

Second victory, I thought.

"You never cease to amaze me, Miguelito," Lucinda said. "Just look at you now. Trying to seduce an older woman? A woman who could be your mother?"

"My mother is still a beautiful woman," I said, looking

over the panorama of cars recently buffed and waxed. "You know that better than I do. And, regarding the other thing," I added, straightening my coffee cup atop the white tablecloth, "please, don't call me Miguelito anymore."

Lucinda smiled, warily.

"Seriously, you never cease to amaze me."

I watched the arm of the parking lot attendant buffing a car as if he were looking for a genie.

Women like alpha males, I thought, like Blondie, the kind with guns who make others do the digging.

"Bring me a glass of water," I said loudly.

And the waiter, who was passing by, went to get one.

We spent the rest of the afternoon flirting, remembering those innocent years when we spent time together in Malinsky's father's house, my uncle's, and the less innocent years afterwards when Malinsky, worried I might get bored with being his only cousin, invited me to spend some time in his home, and I accepted. We were only seven years apart, but at twenty-three and just beginning timidly to thinking about love, the presence, the presence of Lucinda, I mean, got confused with other definitions of affection. She was thirty and had the sort of fondness for me that an older sister would have, she'd let me brush her leg by accident we watched a movie, even though it wasn't an accident. Over time, I said, differences in age tend to shrink: now she was thirty-three years old, a young widow who deserved to make a new life without obstacles. She was tall and willowy, with firm skin accustomed to aerobics, though she'd had always been highly critical of her qualities. And this time I gave free reign to my thoughts: she'd always been beautiful to me, now more than ever, this time it was different. And that's what I said.

She blushed. I could have considered it my third victory of the day, but that's not something the new me would have done: it's something the old me might have thought, the one dying, the one that had already died. So a little urgently then, I realized we had come to a fork in that road and it was time to make a choice, and on my own, without any protective voice, I chose my way. The table separated us in a space that could fit two robust bodies, more or less, and I fearlessly stretched out my hand. Lucinda withdrew hers. I saw her confused, and then distressed. But an hour later, when she stepped out of the car in which I had driven her home, I saw her hesitate, and in the end she didn't reject the contact. It was as if someone, suddenly, had tied a good knot between the two of us.

Lucinda and I never saw the black cat crossing the sidewalk that day, as she had supposed; all we saw was the sunset holding hands, which turned into a custom of ours, and later a strange sort of need. The red above the cliffs, behind our future garden—the one she'd plant and I'd water until the first flowers bloomed—fell like a soft silk backdrop over the two of us, seducing her and on the contrary for me, dropping in a heap over my suffocating brain. I say this with some apprehension. And I say it knowing how little it matters. Because Mr. Munch followed me around then, and whenever that happens, I worry that he'll open his mouth and say something inappropriate that calls me out. He'd been observing me with those severe, dilated yellow eyes of his all afternoon, since Lucinda and I occupied the bed and was relegated to licking a paw on the other side of the apartment.

I'd forgotten about those eyes for a while, but there they were again: those piercing eyes I knew so well, no matter how many times I'd watched their mute indifference, because once I had actually *heard* them, I heard them and could still feel them resonating in the tautness of my arms that never stopped pulling, and in the panting heat of my effort, and exhaustion, the cruel texture forever sunk into the lines in my palms. His eyes, the only things that were real, those big yellow eyes that stared from between the chairs, the eyes that maybe I, too, might have seen pushing my cousin Malinsky into the void from the easy chair. Or was it merely a dream, some perverse effect of his yellow gaze that made me revisit every night what had never happened except in my sweetest dreams?

"Such a beautiful cat," I heard Lucinda say, as if she were three streets away. From the distance, somehow forever, I looked at my hands too, and in them I saw lines

I would never be able to erase. "And to think it was him who had brought us together."

A shiver made its way through my body, like a long line of vigorous ants.

I don't think she noticed what was happening, because soon she grabbed my arm in hers and forced me to walk by her side, with a budding, domestic smile.

"Yeah," I said, to be contrary, knowing beforehand what might take place one day in the not too distant future. Anticipating the unavoidable response, I covered my ears with both hands. And let out a shrill scream, the kind that makes others shake you awake.

CARLOS YUSHIMITO was born in Lima, Peru, in 1977. In 2008 he was chosen as one of the best young writers in Latin America by Casa de las Americas and the Centro Onelio Cardoso de Cuba; and in 2010, by Granta as one of the Best Young Spanish Language Novelists. He recently joined the University of California, Riverside, faculty after receiving a PhD from Brown University.

VALERIE MILES is an American writer, editor, and translator who lives in Barcelona. In 2003, she co-founded Granta en español. She writes and reviews for the *New York Times*, *The Paris Review*, *El País*, *La Nación*, *La Vanguardia*, and *el ABC*, among others.

Transit Books is a nonprofit publisher of international and American literature, based in Oakland, California. Founded in 2015, Transit Books is committed to the discovery and promotion of enduring works that carry readers across borders and communities. Visit us online to learn more about our forthcoming titles, events, and opportunities to support our mission.

TRANSITBOOKS.ORG